I0656960

William Shakespeare, Joseph Hatton

With a Show in the North

Reminiscences of Mark Lemon. Together with Mark Lemon's rev. text of Falstaff.

William Shakespeare, Joseph Hatton

With a Show in the North
Reminiscences of Mark Lemon. Together with Mark Lemon's rev. text of Falstaff.

ISBN/EAN: 9783337105914

Printed in Europe, USA, Canada, Australia, Japan

Cover: Foto ©Andreas Hilbeck / pixelio.de

More available books at **www.hansebooks.com**

CONTENTS.

THE STORY OF FALSTAFF: SELECTED FROM KING
HENRY IV. BY MARK LEMON.

The Author is indebted to the conductors of the *Illus-trated London News* for the Frontispiece. The Portrait was drawn specially for the *News* by John Tenniel, of *Punch*, and it has been copied by photography, and printed by Messrs. Griggs.

With a Show in the North.

REMINISCENCES

OF

MARK LEMON.

BY

JOSEPH HATTON.

[Reprinted from the "Gentleman's Magazine."]

TOGETHER WITH

MARK LEMON'S
REVISED TEXT OF FALSTAFF.

LONDON:

Wm. H. ALLEN & Co., 13, WATERLOO PLACE.

PALL MALL, S.W.

1871.

CHAPTER I.

BEFORE THE PLAY AND AFTER.

A FEW sad words, by way of preface, to some pleasant reminiscences of one of the most genial, kindly, and noble-hearted of God's creatures. Mark Lemon had all the qualities of true greatness. He was modest, unaffected, sympathetic, generous, manly. He never under-estimated any work so much as his own. He was a good husband, an affectionate father, a true friend. He believed in one God, in one woman, in one publication. Simple in his tastes, his ambition was the ambition of every honest man, to be useful to his country and a blessing to his home. In the

1

conduct of *Punch* he soared above the satirist, he repudiated the mere cap and bells. He had a romantic faith in the power which he directed. In this enthusiasm and devotion may be found the secret of his success as an editor. Years hence, it may almost seem beyond belief, that the founder of *Punch* died without deserving the enmity of any man, beloved by all who had laboured with him, respected by men of all creeds and parties; being, nevertheless, one who had never sacrificed the independence of his paper, regarding it always as an estate of the realm, a power that belonged to the country, a national institution.

With a sad yet tender interest I have been looking over a drawer full of Mark Lemon's letters. Amongst his last written words to me, I find an assurance of affection which had been borne in upon me many a time and oft during the last few years. " I wish we lived nearer to each other, for I love you and yours . . . . .

God bless you all!" I reciprocated to the full all his love, and I take it as a patent of good character to have had the esteem and regard of such a man. Amongst his letters I find my notes of a tour with him in the North, the first chapter already transcribed for the press. They were intended to be published during his lifetime, dealing, however, rather more with the general incidents of the tour than with individual details. I recast them now, with a more serious purpose in view than simply to amuse. At the same time, I shall endeavour to retain in them some of the buoyancy of the time, even at the risk of the local colour seeming too powerful in the deep shadow of that sad event which adds to their interest.

Glancing over my notes at this present writing, it is hard to realise the melancholy fact that Mark Lemon is no more; difficult to understand the certainty of the darkness that has gathered about the well-known form and

shut it out from us for ever. It did not fall to
my lot to be present at his funeral; but the
quiet home in the pretty Sussex county rises
up before me as I write. I see the solemn
procession, the sympathising villagers, the old
friends and fellow-workers gathering in the
gloom of the funeral pall. I see the country
churchyard. I stand by a newly-opened grave.
I look down through my tears, and note the
words, "Mark Lemon, Editor of *Punch*," half
covered with flowers strewn by friendly hands
amongst the earthy emblems of mortality,
that made a sad accompaniment to the parson's
parting words, "ashes to ashes, dust to dust.'
Yet memory clings fondly to the living man,
and dismisses, as quickly as sensibility will
permit, this last sad scene of all. I shall make
an effort to get back into the past, though I do
not intend to take you far away from the day
when our dear friend rested from his labours.
The fact that my first chapter was written

several months ago, is a great assistance to me. It carries me at once into the happy holiday-time. There is a pleasant smile in the opening paragraphs which I could never have put there with that last tender message of the dead lying before me : " I love you and yours ; God bless you all."

We called it a show. When I say we, I mean the younger members of the company. Being amateurs, the rakish *abandon* of the term suited our holiday humour. The grave and reverend chief, sweet Jack Falstaff, rare Jack Falstaff, kind Jack Falstaff, smiled benignantly upon our frolicsome notions. He gave himself up to all our whims and fancies. It seemed as if he were trying to be young again. For that matter, he was young ; he had a rich unctuous voice, and a merry catching laugh. We chose to call ourselves strollers. I was the show-

man, the manager, the governor, except when
the leading man, in mock solemnity, dubbed
me the amateur imprcsario. We had no cara-
van, but we had a large quantity of luggage;
more particularly, we had something that
looked like scenery. Our porter called this his
" bag of tricks." The company usually spoke
of it . as " The Show." It was labelled
" Falstaff." The effect of that inscription
was magical everywhere. Railway inspectors,
guards, porters, regarded it almost with vene-
ration. Whenever some experienced and wide-
awake passenger indicated the portly form of
Mark Lemon as the Editor of *Punch*, it was
sure to result in sundry kind enquiries from
the officials with a view to increasing the
amateur actor's comforts while travelling.

My duties commenced very suddenly. The
Show had arrived at Edinburgh before I was
really summoned, as a friend, to take the
management in the absence of the impresario

proper, who was detained in London. "It
will be a holiday for you, there will not be
much work, and I want a pleasant companion."
Falstaff had entered upon his Scottish tour,
and was really waiting to be duly, if not pro-
fessionally, chaperoned through the "land o'
cakes."

I started on a cold morning in 1869 (Ja-
nuary 25) from Euston Square station. It was
ten o'clock when the guard blew his whistle,
and the train moved off on its long, steady,
calm, plodding journey. Thanks to the fact
that well-printed books in large type become
second-hand " sooner or later," I was enabled
to carry away with me as my own property, at
something less than a guinea, the novel of that
name, and I needed no *Times,* nor *Standard,*
nor *Telegraph,* nor any other paper to help the
time along between London and Edinburgh.
When we were once fairly free of the big city,
the train stopped no more until we arrived at

Mugby Junction; and then, sirs, not until we were at Crewe; and then, ladies and gentlemen, not until we came to Preston, where the welcome announcement was made of "twenty minutes allowed for dinner." Travelling from Paris to Vienna, you order your dinner, *en route,* from a carte which the guard brings to you; and at the station where you stop for dinner you find it ready and waiting your arrival, the guard having telegraphed your wishes an hour or so previously. We shall probably never arrive at so high a state of civilisation as this in England; but we travel rapidly and smoothly, and we get fresh foot-warmers and civility on the way, and a real dinner to boot, which is an advance on ten years ago. The Caledonian Railway is not an interesting line, so far as scenery is concerned. Looking up from my book, the chief things I remember are certain highly-illuminated wayside references to "The Daily Telegraph—

Largest Circulation in the World." "Standard—Largest Paper." "Colman's Mustard."
"Families Removing." "Tidman's Sea Salt."
What enormous sums this thorough system of
advertising represents! Writing home, the
next day, to a paper, in which I had an
interest, I said, "Advertise, advertise; newspapers ought to advertise, if only as an example to their clients." We had a hasty
dinner at Preston, and I thought 2*s*. 6*d*. for
the same exceedingly reasonable. An old
Indian officer who travelled with me grumbled
at it; but he was rich, and he grumbled at
everything. He was rich, and had the gout.
His blood was rich, like Bardolph's nose, and
it blazed out all over his face. "Lord Derby
has the gout," he said, "worse than I have."
That seemed to comfort him immensely. He
told me a lion story. All Indians tell lion
stories: it is the thing. When I come home
from India, I shall no doubt have slain as many

lions as other people. My Indian friend was a
real hero, nevertheless. I have no doubt about
it. He growled out some sanguinary incidents
of the mutiny, tending to show how fiercely
the British soldier can take his revenge. That
home blow of " Ernest to Magdalen " had just
been struck in "'Sooner or Later," and my
friend the Indian had just blown twenty
Sepoys from twenty guns, when the train ran
into the railway station at Edinburgh, having
done the journey, including stoppages and
twenty minutes for dinner, in eleven hours.

Within a quarter of an hour after my arrival I
was behind the scenes in the northern city; and in
time to hear the best modern representative of
the fat knight declare, amidst a roar of laughter,
that he was accursed to rob in that thief's
company. "The manager," said my friend
Bardolph, whispering Prince Hal; "the new
manager !" A "super" overheard the remark,
and I was duly installed. I peeped through a hole

in the curtain, saw that there was a good house, went round to the front and announced myself to a member of the enterprising committee which had farmed the show, took a survey of the place, came · back, shook hands with Falstaff in his armour, and went to the Waterloo, pleased with myself and everybody else.

At night, when all was over, we had an actors' supper. Our company at the Waterloo consisted of Falstaff, · Bardolph, Shallow, and Dame Quickly. The Prince, Poins, and the others had apartments elsewhere. They were the professional members of the company. We of the Waterloo were the amateurs, save and except Madame Quickly, who was professional and to the manner born—a clever actress and an excellent hostess, mark you. It was a rare evening. Having fought the battle of the day over again, we lapsed quietly into toddy and anecdote. Falstaff was himself— bright, genial, and witty, full of stories that belong to literary history. He had been amused with two incidents which had occurred on the other side of the border. The gentleman who was playing Chief Justice Shallow, for his own pleasure as well as the public's, hated Jews. It was in truth his favourite hobby to dislike "the chosen people." For my own part, let me confess it at once, I admire the race. Jews are amongst our most intellectual citizens. However, Shallow hated them. A few evenings prior to our chat at the Waterloo, he was in Birmingham playing at billiards. There was present a gentleman of undoubtedly Israelitish extraction, who very rudely offered opinions on the game. "Excuse me," he said, noticing one of Shallow's strokes, "you should have played for the cannon with the left side on your ball." "Thank you," said Shallow; "that may be the style in Judea, but I assure you we play differently in Birmingham." On another occasion Shallow had distinguished himself by a still smarter and more profane *jeu d'esprit*. It was at King's Cross, I think. A great number of Jews were going on a holiday excursion. They were excited about their tickets and places. Some of them were pushing their way rather roughly to the platform. Shallow was amongst the Gentiles, cynical and savage. "Where are you pushing to?" at last he exclaimed, resenting a dig in the side from a Jewish elbow. "What's the matter? One would think you had got another crucifixion in hand." It was very hard, very bitter. There was a Jerroldic ring in the taunt. Falstaff shook his fist solemnly at Shallow, and threatened to forswear his company; but a kindly twinkle in his eye was the signal for unfettered talk. It was always a great relief when the acting was over, and the supper came, with its after-chat round the fire. There were times when Mark Lemon enjoyed the performance as much as his audience did; times when he entered heart and soul into the vagaries of Falstaff, and on this first night in Edinboro' town the play had gone well in every respect.

Mark Lemon had a large sense of humour; and his humour was kindly, it rarely stung— it was satire with a little sugar. On this memorable evening we all talked " shop "—the new shop. We were at the footlights. It was easy to see that Mark was full of sympathy for actors of all degrees. He was fond of talking about the early days of his dramatic writings. He was by no means a bad mimic. In the scene where Falstaff acts the part of Prince Hal, Mark Lemon had been on this occasion particularly successful in imitating the Prince's manner. " I'll tickle you for a young prince," was the opening of this bit of Mark Lemon's humour. He imitated the prince's flourish of his cane and his jerky manner to perfection. I question if the happy prince ever detected the fun, though it amused everybody else. All this was done without any unkindly feeling for the handsome but somewhat inefficient actor, whom Mark Lemon treated with the greatest kindness and consideration; which is more than can be said of Bardolph's (upon this occasion Harry Lemon) treatment of another member of the company. "So and so says I am a promising actor." "Yes," was Bardolph's reply, "you are a *promising* actor, but you never *perform.*"

"You did not say that, Harry?" said the father, interrogatively.

"I did," was the response; "and thought it clever."

"So it was," said Falstaff, smiling; "our prince would do very well if he were not so good looking. It is his firm conviction that some night a coach and six will be waiting outside the stage-door ready to carry him off to be married to an heiress who has been dying for him all through the performance. But for this he would not be a bad actor. It is pleasant to be young and handsome."

Mark Lemon was a handsome man himself, young and old. Latterly he had worn a beard, which well became the part of "Falstaff"—a fine massive beard. His white silvery hair added to the picturesqueness of his make up, more especially in the scene where the fat knight is cast off by the prince, before whom he bends his bared head. Mark Lemon played the part in his own hair and beard. He padded very slightly for it. Beyond this, and a little rouge, he was, in appearance, Falstaff behind the scenes as well as before the footlights.

Mark Lemon's notion of Falstaff developed a far more considerate feeling for the fat knight's frailties than is generally entertained. He was ever ready to discuss Shakspeare's intentions with regard to this particular character.

"Shakspeare is not to blame for making Falstaff use language which we feel called upon to exclude from our drawing-room version. It was the language of the time. Look in any other playwright's works, and see what others did. They give you indecency for indecency's sake, lewdness without wit, filth without humour."

"Is not that the modern fashion?" asked Shallow. "I was talking with a countryman of mine who seemed to wonder that you could make Falstaff respectable."

"Falstaff respectable! He was a gentleman, Shallow; and would thou wert as well furnished with brains."

"Thank you," said Shallow, "I know not how I may improve, unless you lend me your doublet, Sir John, and stuff me out with straw."

"Ha! ha!" laughs Bardolph, "if that be *apropos* or witty I'm a shotten herring."

"I'll anoint thy face and call thee horse, an thou callest me anything but an honest man," says Shallow.

These two members of the Falstaff company hardly ever conversed, except in the language of the little book, price sixpence, being Mark Lemon's version of Falstaff, in which the fat knight was purified and made wholesome.

"Falstaff was a gentleman," says Mark Lemon, "fallen away, in the general degeneracy of the times, from the path of rectitude; but, nevertheless, a gentleman. He was not a buffoon. Poor old —— (mentioning an actor of considerable reputation) was quite outraged because I would not go down on my face and grovel in the robbery scene."

"That is the recognised legitimate business," I remark.

"Granted! It is not the only business to which I object, on principle. Like Falstaff, I am fat and growing old, heaven help the wicked! and I might have as great a difficulty in getting up again, being down, as poor Jack had. He was no buffoon."

"An awful liar, though," says Bardolph.

"A cowardly knave," says Mistress Quickly, who had been invited to sup with us, having played the Dame to perfection.

"A spendthrift, and one who did not pay his just debts—that five hundred, to wit," says Shallow.

"His lies were, for the most part, white lies," replies the editor of *Punch;* "mostly white lies, my masters."

"The buckram men, for example," suggests Bardolph.

"Yes, the men in buckram suits," sayeth our leader. "He saw almost immediately that the Prince knew all: he exaggerated his first fib that he might make the affair the more ridiculous, piling up the fun until that grand climax, 'By the Lord I knew ye!' And mark how he chaffed the Lord Chief Justice. There is no part of the play that sparkles more with Shakspeare's genius than Falstaff's interview, with the Chief Justice in the second scene of the first act. 'To wake.a wolf is as bad as to smell a fox.' "

" But he was a hard man; he behaved cruelly to Mistress Quickly," remarks the lady.

" Yes, Dame, he was; but not harder than others. The times were out of joint. He was a gentleman of the period; had he lived in these days he would have been a different man. And then he was so very hard up! But Mistress Quickly loved the rogue for all that. There is nothing to my mind more affecting than her description of Falstaff's death. 'He parted even just between twelve and one, e'en at the turning o' the tide; I saw him fumble with the sheets, and play with flowers, and smile upon his fingers' ends; he babbled of green fields.' "

The thought of this glimpse of Falstaff's mind wandering back to his days of inno- cency always seemed to impress Mark Le-

mon with the correctness of his liberal judgment of Falstaff's character.

On this particular evening the contemplation
of the poor knight's death evidently set the
critic thinking of others who had gone out
with the tide; for when Bardolph and the rest
were abed, and the waiter had received a
kindly shake of the head in response to the
inquiry if we wanted anything else, the editor
and actor began to talk of Hood, and Jerrold
and Leech.

"Poor Hood," he said; "when he sent me
his 'Song of the Shirt,' he accompanied it with
a few lines, in which he expressed a fear that
it was hardly suitable for *Punch*, leaving it
between my discretion and the waste-basket."

"It created a profound sensation," I suggested.

"Yes; we received letters from all parts of
the country. The sale of the number was
enormous, I believe."

"Yet, to be fully appreciated, he had to do one thing, as Douglas Jerrold puts it in his preface to 'Cakes and Ale:' that one thing was—to die."

"It is generally so," he replied; "though, for that matter, Leech and Thackeray were appreciated during their lives; and Dickens, there is success for you! I am glad Dickens sent me that kind note and message the other day."

There had been an estrangement between Charles Dickens and Mark Lemon, which the great master of fiction had brought to an end by some kindly message when the Editor of *Punch* was announced as Falstaff. In early life, Mark Lemon and Dickens were intimate friends and neighbours. They were both members of that amateur company which played, years ago, for the benefit of the Guild of Literature and Art. The Editor of *Punch* had walked with Dickens, more than once, to scenes selected by the novelist for delineation in his works. Mark Lemon had the greatest admiration for his old friend's genius.

" I hope you have really made memoranda of the history of *Punch*," I said.

" I have made a few notes," he replied; " I shall tell the story of *Punch*, I hope, and I shall do it without wounding any one."

" It is due to literature, to the profession, to your family, that you should write that history. The other day I saw a lecture announced professing to be the true story of *Punch* and its contributors."

" No one can tell that but myself. *Punch* was started in a very humble way. It was kept alive on two occasions by the success of two little plays of mine, the money for which went to pay the printer; one play was called *Punch*, the other *The Silver Thimble*. This was, of course, before we took it to Bradbury and Evans."

I think there were three of the staff who waited upon the old firm of Bradbury and Evans to offer them the copyright of *Punch*. One was Mark Lemon; another Douglas Jerrold. I do not remember the name of the third. Mark Lemon did the editing for a ridiculously small honorarium. The publication was in debt to the publishers nearly £8000 before it paid a penny.

"It was our first Christmas Number that made the fortune of *Punch*; and, when it was once prosperous, we never looked back again."

By this time Falstaff had just finished his last pipe, and we bade each other good night.

"By the way," he said, "I know you like reading before you go to bed, here's a penance for you. Read this, and tell me what you think of it in the morning. Let us be up betimes; we will have a carriage, and see Edinburgh. Good-night—God bless you!"

The MS. he gave me was a chapter of a new novel not yet published. It was to be called "The Taffeta Petticoat." The manuscript has been in the hands of the printer for some months. I read the chapter; it was the description of a Fair, and admirably done. Mark Lemon's best novel is "Faulkner Lyle;" his best play, "Hearts are Trumps;" his best song, "Old Time and I," the first copy of which I had brought that day from London. There was an old piano in the hotel, and I tried Walter Maynard's music over for him. I venture to reprint the words :—

> Old Time and I the other night
>   Had a carouse together;
> The wine was golden, warm, and bright,—
>   Aye! just like summer weather.
> Quoth I, " Here's Christmas come again,
>   And I no farthing richer;"
> Time answered, " Ah, the old, old strain !—
>   I prithee pass the pitcher."

" Why measure all your good in gold ?
　　No rope of sand is weaker ;
　Tis hard to got, 'tis hard to hold—
　　Come, lad, fill up your beaker."
" Hast thou not found true friends more true,
　　And loving ones more loving ?"
　I could but say, " A few, a few !
　　So keep the liquor moving."

" Hast thou not seen the prosp'rous knave
　　Come down a precious thumper ?
　His cheats disclosed," " I have, I have !"
　　" Well, surely that's a bumper !"
" Nay, hold awhile, I've seen the just
　　Find all their hopes grow dimmer."
" 'They will hope on, and strive, and trust,
　　And conquer !"　" That's a brimmer."

" 'Tis not because to-day is dark,
　　No brighter day's before 'em ;
　There's rest for every storm-tossed bark ;"
　　" So be it !　Pass the jorum !"
" Yet I must own, I should not mind
　　To be a little richer."
" Labour and wait, and you may find——"
　　" Halloah ! an empty pitcher."

There is undeniable poetic fancy and philosophy in this effective ballad, as there is in many of the songs, too little known, from the same pen.

In these loose notes the reader will find no attempt to tell the story of Mark Lemon's life. There is a memoir, I believe, in preparation. Carefully written, such a work will be of great interest; it will, to a large extent, be a history of letters and journalism for the last thirty years. If these papers of mine should in any way assist the memory of Mark Lemon's biographer, or throw any light upon the latter days of an eventful life, I shall feel that my notes will have rendered the State some service.

CHAPTER II.

A RAMBLE ON WHEELS.

"I LIKE the chapter much," I said, the next morning, handing my friend the MS. which he had placed in my hands over night.

"Is it too long?"

"No."

"I don't pretend to be a descriptive writer. I hope this may be my last effort."

"I am not sure that I like your title."

"'The Taffeta Petticoat?' I thought it rather novel. The story all turns upon the colour and character of that particular article of dress."

"Of all the titles of your works, I like more than any other that of *Hearts are Trumps.*"

"Did I ever tell you how the story suggested itself to me?"

"Yes; but I have an imperfect recollection of the incident. You shall give me a second edition of it, if you will."

"By-and-by; when we are reposing comfortably in our chariot."

Here we are interrupted by Bardolph and Shallow, who come in to breakfast, with the daily papers (containing notices of the performance of the previous night), and letters for "Falstaff." These latter are of far deeper interest to Sir John than the papers, which Bardolph and Shallow eagerly devour, extolling this editor in mock heroics, and damning with faint praise the other. Shallow pretends to be very bitter against the press for the ignominious way in which he is overlooked. We have a smart discussion upon the equivocal compliments which Bardolph receives for the " make-up of his nose."

" That nose of thine," remarks Shallow, " seems to get into the editorial head."

" I would it were in the editorial stomach."

" Ah, then indeed would the press be heart-burned," responds Shallow. " Sir John Falstaff, a word with you."

" Ah, Shallow, give you good time of day," says Mark Lemon, looking up from his letters. " Shall we to breakfast? Give me a cup of coffee."

Thus breakfast commences, accompanied by a rattle of harmless fun and apt Falstaffian quotation. The end of the morning meal brings the carriage ordered over night. Bardolph and Shallow leave us, to explore Edinburgh on foot. Falstaff and the amateur impresario are of a lazier habit of body. The holiday feeling has taken too firm a hold upon them for anything but an idle, lolling, easy, dreamy indulgence on wheels.

We were fortunate in obtaining the services of a particularly intelligent driver, who was evidently proud of his fare.

"Tell us all you know," said Mark Lemon, as he got into the conveyance; "tell us all you know, and stop at any place of special interest. When you have driven us where you please, then we will direct you. We have a call to make."

The coachman obeyed these instructions with great tact and judgment. Whether he told us all he knew, or more, is neither here nor there. He was an excellent showman, and the little present of "Falstaff," with some kindly words of remembrance written therein, and signed "Mark Lemon," which he carried home that day, will now, alas! more than ever be a cherished memorial of Mark Lemon's visit to Scotland.

Sandy pointed to the unfinished monument on Calton Hill as "the national disgrace." At the Castle he gave us an example of his reading and intelligence by his shrewd reference to the stratagem by which Sir William Douglas recovered possession of the place in 1341. A party of Sir William's men, dressed as sailors, arrived early in the morning at the Castle gate with a cartload of wine, which they said had just arrived by land at Leith. They upset the cart in the middle of the gate. This prevented the portcullis from being lowered. A number of men, who had been placed in ambuscade during the night, rushing in to the assistance of the sailors, the garrison was put to the sword, and possession of the Castle regained.

It is a grand historical romance, the history of Edinburgh Castle. The past and present are characteristically united on the Castle Hill by a monumental cross to the officers of the

78th Highlanders who fell in the Crimea. There are some curious old buildings here. A cannon ball still sticks in the side of a house which originally belonged to the Marquis of Huntly. This suggestive memorial of the past no doubt found its present resting-place during that stormy time when the Castle was held for the King by General Grant, while the town and Holyrood were in possession of Prince Charles.

From Castle Hill you get a fine view of the Grass Market, the site of public executions in the old days. Captain John Porteous was hanged here to a dyer's pole. His crime was that of intercepting an attempt at rescue during the execution of a smuggler. He fired upon the mob without warning. He was pardoned by the king, but the people seized the officer and hanged him. The incident is graphically narrated in the "Heart of Mid-

3

lothian." There is still a cross on the pave-
ment where the gallows stood.

A topographical or historic notice of the
district is quite outside the pale of this paper;
but there are a few incidents of general
interest which I venture to print in this place,
some of which Sandy told us, some of which
we marked in our " Murray's Guide." For-
merly butter and provisions were weighed
before they were allowed to come into the city.
The weigh-house was at the top of West Bow,
but in 1822 it was removed to make room for
the public entry of George IV. Lord Ruth-
ven lived in the West Bow. The street was
the head-quarters of the Covenanter party,
and at the same time was occupied chiefly by
smiths and pewterers. It was from this
association that the Covenanters got the name
of the Bowhead saints. In James Court was
the house of David Hume, and afterwards that

of James Boswell, who entertained Johnson there in 1773. The house was burnt down in 1859. In the Covenanter's Close was situated a tavern much frequented by lawyers in the days of Sir Walter Scott. It was here that the Solemn League and Covenant was placed for signature in 1840.

Finding my companion, Sir John, suddenly raising his hat in the street, and seeing no response from the window to which his eyes were directed, I found that he was doing homage to a quaint old gabled house, projecting into a narrow street. It was John Knox's house, upon which is inscribed, "Lofe God abofe al things, and yi neighbours as yiself." At the corner there is a figure of the reformer preaching to the people. Knox narrowly escaped assassination in this house from a shot fired at him through the window. He died here in 1572. The respect which the Scotch show for their great men is in striking contrast to the disregard of the English for houses and places which should be sacred to the memories of men who have made themselves and their country famous throughout the world. The poet Gay lived in Edwin Street, during the latter part of his life, in the capacity of secretary to the Duchess of Queensbury. He resided at Queensbury House, which was then a beautiful building. It was dismantled in 1801, and is now used as a house of refuge.¶

At Holyrood we found a guide as clever and intelligent as our cabman. We had not stood within the shadow of the abbey many minutes before the discreet and appreciative Scot in charge asked if he had not the honour of speaking to Falstaff.

"You have," said Mark Lemon, bowing to the guide, and addressing him in his blandest manner.

No fat man ("a gross fat man, fat as

butter," Mark Lemon has written himself down in sundry albums) ever carried himself more gracefully than my companion. The wave of his hand in a friendly adieu was quite regal. His manner was charmingly sympathetic, and more especially with young people. Children and dogs were always his friends. It was indeed a characteristic of the old *Punch* men, their love of children, and the youthful fashion of their amusements. Leap-frog and rounders were popular games with Jerrold and Dickens.

"I am proud and delighted to see you, Sir," said the keeper of the abbey, "you have afforded me many an hour's pleasure through your famous publication. If you will allow me, Sir, to present you with a photograph of the abbey, my happiness will be increased."

"Your words gratify me much," said Mark Lemon; "permit me to offer you a card in return."

"Thank you, Sir; you may rely on it I shall come and see you to-night and bring my family." ·

Further compliments were exchanged, and we had a fund of information from the attendant concerning Holyrood. As, however, there is nothing more to be said about the place than has been said before, I venture to leave it in the hands of my readers, who can easily get up the history for themselves. Mark Lemon was particularly interested in the Rizzio incident. We planned out the tragedy in detail, as hundreds had done before us, and without quite satisfying ourselves upon all the historical particulars of the murder. We certainly did not believe in that sanguinary-looking stain on the stairs, though we were deeply impressed by the industry of the single artist whose single brush had done so much in the portrait decorations of the picture gallery.

"Hepworth Dixon should tell the story of Holyrood," I remarked.

"It is worth doing," said Mark Lemon; "but what we want, in sketches of a place like this, in addition to the mere written history of the past, are the recollections of some old and observant man who has lived near it all his life. Just imagine what I could tell in my short time about London. The changes which have taken place within my memory are marvellous. It would make an interesting volume; and be additionally attractive, done in a sort of Rip Van Winkle style. Let a man go to sleep in his own house, say fifty years ago, under mysterious circumstances that could be worked out; let him be awakened now, send him forth, and let him recount by the light of half a century ago the changes that had gone on during his trance."

It had always been one of Mark Lemon's fondest hopes, that before he died he would

have time to write his personal recollections of
London. He made an important step in this
direction when he prepared and delivered his
lectures on London, which afterwards appeared
in *London Society,* and were finally made up
into a pleasant book (which has gone through
one large edition), called "Up and Down the
London Streets." I call to mind a notable
Sunday spent with the author in Bedford
Street, and some curious topographical incidents, which I hope to reproduce in my next
chapter.

Meanwhile we rattle down the streets of
Edinburgh, and alight for luncheon at the
"Waterloo," where we find half-a-dozen
albums with polite requests for autographs.
Amongst these is an interesting book from the
guide, who had been so attentive to Falstaff at
Holyrood. There are several cards upon our
table, one of them has been left by Mr.
Russell, the editor of *The Scotsman,* a distin-

guished journalist, who a few years ago received at the hands of his fellow citizens a splendid testimonial of their esteem. Mr. Russell is a remarkable man, his journal is in the foremost rank of newspapers. An account of the management of *The Scotsman* would form a particularly interesting chapter in the history of journalism. Through a special telegraph wire, the paper is supplied by its own staff in London with a daily report of Parliament. An excellent summary of the debate of each night may be found on the Edinburgh breakfast tables the next morning. There is no more noteworthy evidence of the enterprise and ability which characterise the management of the provincial press in these days, than the striking equality of the information contained in a London paper and a journal published several hundred miles away from the metropolis. *The Scotsman* sometimes even anticipates London with a piece of

important news. *The Irish Times* is frequently in advance of its London namesake.
The Newcastle Daily Chronicle had a special
train from London to convey its reporters
from a recent boat-race on the Thames.
During the visit of the British Association,
the proprietors engaged a whole staff of
London press men, essayists, and short-hand
writers, that the fullest justice might be done
to the wise men and their sayings. I might
mention a dozen other newspapers equally
deserving, and I should do so if this were a
treatise on provincial journalism, which it is
not. The country press wants an historian.
He would have an entertaining and instructive
story to tell. The oldest-established newspapers are in the provinces, and some of them
have had famous men as editors. De Quincey,
I believe, conducted a paper in Cumberland.
Many of our best men in London made their
first appearances in country newspapers.

Mark Lemon wrote his first paragraph for *The Stamford Mercury.* He spent some years of his early life in Lincolnshire.

After luncheon we received a visit from Mr. Peter Fraser, who is well known in the literary circles of Edinburgh. In his agreeable society we returned a call from Mr. Edmonston, of the well-known publishing firm. Mr. Fraser thought it a coincidence worth mentioning, that having recently been appointed a justice of the peace, his first official act was to assist in granting a license for the performance of Falstaff by his old friend, Mark Lemon. Mr. Fraser talked of former days when Mark Lemon visited Scotland for the first time. It was during the appearance of the amateur actors who played for the Guild of Literature and Art, under the auspices of Sir Edward Bulwer Lytton. The justice called to mind a red-letter evening at Liverpool, during that famous tour, when Dickens was particularly bright, and genial, and humorous. The author of "Pickwick" in those days was a lithe, active man, full of nervous energy and physical power. On this red-letter evening he gave his friends a never-to-be-forgotten instance of his athletic skill, by jumping over the broad back of his brother player, Mark Lemon. Sir John Falstaff remembered the incident, and laughed heartily, as other memories of those happy days came back to him.

"It was hard work, though," he remarked, shaking his head, "harder than Falstaff; I often had to rush off to town by a mail train, starting immediately after the performances, and get back again to play the next night."

Mark Lemon wished to see the literary sanctuary of "Old Ebony." Mr. Fraser and Mr. Edmonston thereupon accompanied us to the office of *Blackwood's Magazine*. The room, the table and chairs, used by Chris-

topher North, Wilson, Lockhart, Hogg, and
the famous band of Scotch authors, are still
preserved. The editor of *Punch*, with unaffected reverence, sat in the editorial chair,
surrounded by portraits of the great men who
had taken sweet counsel together in the past.
The founder of *Punch* in "Old Ebony's"
private room might furnish a suggestive text
for a ready writer possessing a well-stored
memory of the literary history of the past half
century.

"You cannot wonder at the Scotch being a
proud race, vain of their country, and of
Edinburgh in particular," said Falstaff, when
he and I were once more alone, and had taken
up our shrewd cabman again for another
short drive before going to the scene of the
evening's performance, "What a grand city it
is! What rare citizens!"

"Full of literary feeling," I said.

"None more so," he replied; "what

tributes to literature are their monuments of Scott and Burns."

"This is Sir Walter Scott's house," said the driver, pulling up opposite a substantial, unobtrusive residence.

"Thanks, my man," said Falstaff, quietly raising his hat to the house; "the greatest genius of this century, sir!"

"As a poet?" I asked.

"Both as poet and romance writer."

"It is a question whether his stories in verse would not have been better done in prose."

. "A matter of opinion," said Falstaff; "I do not hold it. There is a fashion in depreciating Scott's poetry. 'The Lady of the Lake' and 'Marmion' are fine specimens, nevertheless."

An incident of Canongate made a great impression upon my friend. Some few years ago a block of houses fell here, killing thirty-six people. When the workmen had almost despaired of rescuing a boy who was still almost miraculously alive beneath a weight of bricks and timber, a little voice suddenly urged them on to fresh exertions: "Heave away, chaps, I'm no deed yet," said the little voice, quite cheerily. In rebuilding the houses the lad has been immortalised. The principal doorway is adorned with his bust. His own brave words are written beneath it. The Scotch never held up to the world a more striking example of their courage and patience.

"I have seen nothing in all Edinburgh that has touched me more than that bust in Canongate," said the amateur actor when we reached the hotel.

Before we went to the Hall Mark Lemon repeated to me his story of the origin of *Hearts are Trumps*, a drama which was very successful in its day, and might be brought back to the stage with advantage just now. I am not quite clear as to the exact details, but if my memory serves me, Mark Lemon's words were to the following purpose :—

"One day I went to see an old friend of mine, —— the actor (mentioning the name of a popular and deservedly-respected comedian). In a corner of the room sat a gentleman, rather dilapidated in the matter of dress, yet in his way a presentable, respectable-looking person, not over fifty. What struck me more particularly about the man was his white hair. He was not an old man, but his hair was as white as the tresses of Scott's Last Minstrel. My friend —— did not introduce me, and presently the white-haired decayed gentleman left, the actor shaking hands with him and taking quite an affectionate farewell. When the stranger had gone, my friend said, 'Excuse me, Mark, that is ——, the gambler, I never introduce him to my friends; but he comes here whenever he pleases. When I was a

young man and struggling hard in my profession, he was very kind to me, and I never
forget kind actions; he is down on his luck
now, hard up, and comes here to have a
meal whenever he wants one.' The incident
haunted me. 'And that is ——, is it?' I said
to myself as I walked home. What a career, I
thought; and then I began to revolve him in
my mind with a view to 'copy.' He was a
benevolent-looking man, not at all like a
gambler, not at all the sort of fellow I should
have taken for ——. I wondered if he were
married, if he had a daughter, and if they
knew what his profession was. Then it
occurred to me to build up the story of a
gambler who had a daughter living away from
town in happy ignorance of her father's career.
And this is how it came about that I wrote the
play of *Hearts are Trumps,* which you are
pleased to say is so excellent a drama. There
is another curious circumstance connected with

4

that play. One evening I was at the Adelphi
Theatre with Charles Dickens. During the
performance I noticed the gambler in the pit.
' Look, Dickens,' I said presently, ' there is my
leading man in *Hearts are Trumps*—there is
the fellow I told you of ! It seemed to me
that I would like to speak to him. Strange
to say his make-up was just like the make-up
in my piece. I went round to the pit and
sent a message to the man. He came out and
I mentioned the incident of seeing him at
——. I was mistaken. The man in the pit
was the brother of the gambler."

Mr. Mark Lemon's treatment of Falstaff was
novel in every respect. In the first place he
selected scenes from parts I. and II. of *Henry
IV.* in such a way as to make a consistent
story of the fat knight's career, from the hey-
day of his friendship with Prince Hal to the
period when he is cast off and condemned to
the Fleet. This bringing together of the prin-

cipal scenes in which Falstaff and his more
immediate companions take part, is not unlike
the development of a new play out of two
dramas, without tampering with the text beyond the excision of dialogue which could not
well be spoken in the present day. The play
was the story of Falstaff, his fun and folly, his
amours, his breaches of the law, his robberies,
his soldiering, his lies, his guzzling, and finally
his downfall, his humiliation, his punishment.
Not alone in the acting, but in the compila-
tion of the text did Mark Lemon secure the
sympathy of his audience for Prince Hal's
lawless, but genial companion. Sir John's
impersonation of the King wins the reader's
admiration, his clever scramble through the
Gadshill difficulty gives happy evidence of his
wit, and the reader's good opinion of his skill
in controversial fence is confirmed by his encounter with the Lord Chief Justice. These
scenes gradually build up a sympathetic in-

terest in the knight's welfare, and Mark
Lemon availed himself of all this to give a
pathetic turn to the closing incidents of Sir
John's banishment and arrest by the same
Chief Justice, who had come off second best
in that battle of words, which Mark Lemon
thought the best part of the play.

The arrangements of the stage were as novel
as the selection of the text. There was no
scenery. The only furniture was just such
chairs and tables as were necessary for the
interior of a room. It was announced in the
programme that "the stage would be hung
with tapestry only, as in the days of Shakespeare." There are various authorities for
this. It is generally believed that, in the early
days of the Elizabethan drama, the simple
expedient of printing upon placards the names
of the places where the scenes were laid, served
for scenery. Acting upon this tradition Mark
Lemon had the back of his stage hung with

tapestry. Instead of the curtain falling between each act, a quaintly dressed attendant
came on and renewed the placard upon the
tapestry. For example, when the piece commenced the locality was indicated by a placard
(printed and prepared so as to be somewhat in
character with the tapestry), which informed
the audience that the scene was "An Apartment belonging to the Prince of Wales." This
was followed in due course with "The Road by
Gadshill," and so on to the end of the play.
Everywhere this arrangement acted as an
agreeable surprise, and nowhere more so than
in Edinburgh, where the compact little stage
had an unusually pretty appearance from the
front of the house.

It is not my intention to offer a criticism
upon Mark Lemon's performance of Falstaff.
In the early days of the entertainment, when
the actor was not thoroughly master of the
dialogue, his acting lacked finish. The effort

of memory necessary for a correct rendering of the text interfered with the development and execution of the attendant business.   It was not until the first dozen nights were over that Mark Lemon seemed to grasp the character and master it.   His best performances were in Scotland, and for my own part I cannot imagine a more intelligent or complete impersonation of Shakespeare's fat knight than Mark Lemon's Falstaff.   No longer nervous about verbal imperfections in his reading, he gave up the full bent of his genius to the lights and shades of the character.   With suitable and appropriate action for every word, Sir John Falstaff lived in Mark Lemon, whose physique gave him special advantages over contemporary actors of this arduous and most difficult part. I have said before that there were nights when Mark Lemon heartily enjoyed his work. Several such I remember when he kept up the fun, and jest, and animation of the night in the

green room as well as on the stage, calling
his companions mad-wags, and pint-pots, and
tickle-brains, and asking for cups of sack in
the true Falstaffian fashion. Other nights,
other feelings. Now and then he would weary
of the dressing. The tax of putting on his
armour and lacing his jerkin irritated him, and
sent him before the footlights, "just a peg too
low," as he would afterwards describe his feelings. He rarely drank anything more than a
little brandy and water, or two glasses of port
wine, between the acts, and he found his
greatest solace at the close in a pipe of to-
bacco. Although he had a quick and correct
ear for poetic rhythm, and wrote ballads with
facility, he was not very fond of music. He
would listen with evident pleasure to any
familiar strain, and he enjoyed a song with
thorough enjoyment; but he disliked what he
called " classical fireworks " on the piano, and
it often annoyed him during the Falstaff en-

tertainment to hear some strange pianoforte-
player exhibiting his powers of execution
instead of playing pleasant and appropriate
music to finish or introduce the scenes.
He revenged himself with a hearty laugh at
the expense of one of these gentlemen, who
asked Bardolph to explain to him why Falstaff
was so cut up at being ordered to the Fleet.
"Surely an appointment in the fleet, say
admiral for example, was not so bad a thing."
The innocent musician could not credit the
King with any harsher treatment of his old
friend than banishment as an officer on board a
man-of-war.

It will be interesting in this place to introduce Mark Lemou's explanation with reference
to the Falstaff entertainment. Here are his
own words, reprinted from the programme of
the play :—

"Those who know me will acquit me of the
vanity of unduly desiring to bring my name

before the public, and also of the perhaps less pardonable vanity of supposing myself justified in announcing a series of public appearances by a belief that I have conceived, and can execute, a new and complete presentment of a wonderful dramatic creation. The kindly judgment of my personal friends will unhesitatingly reject both ideas, and it is not to them that I deem it necessary to submit a few words in reference to the undertaking upon which I have, not unreluctantly, ventured. But to the many to whom I am known only as an author, or as the editor of *Punch*, and also to many who may do me the honour to witness the effort which I am about to make, I desire to say a word in explanation of the motives that have prompted me to what might otherwise be considered a certain presumption.

"I have from time to time devoted much study to the great Shakespearean character, Falstaff. I was originally induced to examine it for the purpose of acting its merely comic portion, in association with some of the most brilliant amateur artists I have ever known, who thought me qualified to assist them in a performance of the *Merry Wives of Windsor*. Imperfect as may have been my conception of the part, the labour which I gave to it gradually opened to me some views of the entire purpose and meaning of the character, and these have at no time since failed to occupy my leisure. Upon them I have had the great pleasure and advantage of taking the judgment of many whose names are household words with the nation. But that my ideas have found in the circle I speak of (to whose cordial support and co-operation in my literary career I am proud to avow that I owe a far greater success than I could have attained unaided) a thoughtful recognition and an earnest approval, I should have resisted even longer than I have done, the invitations which have been made to me to present my conception of Falstaff to a larger audience. I have now assented to the tempting propositions that have been made to me, and I have authorised the announcement of the appearances, the details of which are appended.

" It is due to the public to say that I am fully aware of the nature of the arduous task I am undertaking : it is no less due to myself to say that were I not justified by the encouragement and counsels of many whose opinions are entitled to public deference, I should not have presented myself before an audience. But I am not without confidence in the earnestness with which I have addressed myself to my work, and that confidence justifies my adding that, in any circumstances, health and strength permitting, I shall complete the entire series of performances announced by those who have charge of its business arrangements."

The costume in which the editor of *Punch*

dressed the part of Falstaff was specially designed for him by his dear friend and fellow-labourer, John Tenniel, who drew that excellent portrait of "Mark Lemon as Falstaff," which appeared in the *Illustrated London News* shortly after the first representation at the Gallery of Illustration.

CHAPTER III.

GLASGOW AND GREENOCK.

THE public has been so long accustomed to hear of literary men dying without making provision for their families, that an exception to the rule is quoted with congratulatory emphasis. The leading papers have in this spirit recorded the fact that Mark Lemon had insured his life for six thousand pounds. This is true : but it is questionable whether his family will reap any benefit from this thoughtful provision. While Dickens's will deals with eighty thousand pounds, and serves as the text of a sermon at Westminster Abbey, Mark Lemon's will is not to be proven. The truth is, that somehow or another the policies of insurance are claimed by persons outside the family circle. Mark Lemon died a poor man, and it would be false delicacy to disguise this very painful faet. No man worked harder to leave his family " well provided for." Perhaps no man was more unfortunate. He invested moneys in useful and important schemes, which were unsuccessful. His losses were very great in various ways. When the story of his life comes to be told, we shall know how thoroughly, by pen and pursc, Mark Lemon tried, while increasing his income, to serve his country. He never touched anything in a selfish spirit. The schemes by which he lost money were in the interest of art and humanity. His endeavours to rccoup himself on account of these losses were incessant, though he might have succeeded by one single engagement, had he chosen to leave *Punch* and taken his Falstaff entertainment to America. I trust

the Government, having regard to the services
which Mark Lemon rendered to the State, not
only as the editor of *Punch,* but as a dramatist
and a writer in the field of general literature,
will place his devoted widow upon that "roll of
honour" which is thrice adorned when it receives the name of one dear to a useful toiler
who has rested from his labours.

It has been happily said, "When Reality
becomes a foe, it is not unwise to seek a friend
in Fancy." Defeated hope and unfortunate
chances have given to the world many noble
works, many rare entertainments. Sterne told
us in his "Sentimental Journey" that when
his way was too rough for his feet, or too steep
for his strength, he got off it to some smooth
velvet path, which Fancy had scattered over
with rosebuds of delight, and having taken a
few turns on it, came back strengthened and
refreshed. It was this same feeling which
gave us many of Mark Lemon's prettiest

ballads; it crops out unrestrained and plaintive in "Old Time and I;" and the public are indebted to it for the glimpse which Mark Lemon gave us of Falstaff as he understood Shakespeare's conception. Latterly Mark Lemon was not a writer by mere choice, nor an actor from the love of it. He wrote often, as many others do, for recreation as well as for money; he played Falstaff with the strong hope in his heart of leaving his family an independent fortune. One or two critics questioned his taste in coming before the public as reader or actor. Except in the *Saturday Review*, in a recent article on Dickens (dragged from it by the utter insanity of some of the great man's worshippers), I never met with any adverse criticism directed against Thackeray, or Dickens, or Dr. Russell, for giving readings. Mark Lemon, in his own modest estimation of himself, was a far humbler man than either of these, and it must have been a peculiarly-organised mind that could see an outrage on good taste in his ascending the platform as a "reader in costume."

It was not vanity, it was not greed that induced the editor of *Punch* to appear upon the stage. He was influenced by the highest and best motives. Let these and his success in the part selected for exhibition be his justification. I know of no man, holding a leading place in the ranks of literature and journalism, who would so readily have withdrawn himself into private life as Mark Lemon, if the responsibilities of his position could have been reduced so as to have admitted of retirement. A man of simple tastes and moderate ambition, Mark Lemon was happiest when at home in his unpretentious cottage at Crawley, or wandering among the unsophisticated villagers. His next-door neighbour was his own mother, to whom he was ever an affectionate and considerate son. He always made a point of

5

spending his Sunday mornings with her. While his family were at church, Mark Lemon read the New Testament to his mother. He was essentially a religious man. Like most of his literary brethren, he had a wholesome hatred of cant and pretentious religious professions. Perhaps his jealousy of what he called "the simple faith" taught by our Saviour made him just a little intolerant of that class of people who seem, without intending it, to make a parade of their religion. He rarely attended any place of worship; he hated creeds and formularies; but he showed the greatest respect for the Church, and might, with judicious treatment, have been brought to head his family in the family pew. One of the local clerics had, however, seriously displeased him, and he was irritated by theological controversies. "Sir," he said to a friend, "I am so sick of these discussions, so unsettled by disunion in the Church, that I just spread my bit of carpet in a corner, and say my prayers in my own way." It was his custom always to gather his family round him every morning after breakfast, and read a chapter in the New Testament. I see him now, his grey silken hair thrown back from his massive head, with his wife and girls about him, and I hear his deep, sympathetic voice repeating part of that wonderful story of the Man of Sorrows.

It was a quaint, old-fashioned room, the dining-room at Crawley. The main portion of Vine Cottage had once been a farm-house, and it was Mark Lemon's fancy to retain the ingle-nook and some of the old-fashioned characteristics of the place. I remember a particularly notable gathering round the old table by the ingle-nook. Mark Lemon was looked upon as a sort of father of the village. Nothing was done in the place without his advice first taken, and his assistance

secured.   On   the   occasion   in   question   it
was   a   volunteer   fire   brigade.   This   had   the
father's   entire   approval;   and   to   evince   his
sympathy   all   the   more   strongly,   he   had   a
committee meeting at his own house, and what
is   more,   he   invited   the   committee—two   or
three of the most active spirits in Crawley—to
dinner.   Afterwards,   in   the   shadow   of   the
ingle-nook, he gave himself up to the entertainment of his humble and delighted guests.
He   discussed   the   question   of   fire-brigades
generally,   talked   of   the   early   days   of   the
volunteer movement, and turning to me spoke
of their local efforts in this direction, to the
intense enjoyment of his brother volunteers.
" I   could   never   dress   up   properly,"   he   said.
" If   the   dressing   in   front   was   good,   I   always
put   the   company   out   behind.   They   allowed
me   to   have   a   special   tunic,   a   little   longer   than
the rest, but I was obliged to give up drilling;
and   on   the   whole   it   was   decided   that   I   pre-

sented too much of a mark for the enemy to be
of any practical good in the field." I forget
what song the genial father of the village
sung, but it was a humorous effort of the old
school. On second thoughts, I remember me:
it was "Cupid's Garden." The tune was a
jumble of the vocalist's own invention. His
daughters went into the adjoining room, and
gave us some delightful music during the evening; and when the fire brigade had left, Mrs.
Lemon, sitting by the ingle, and without any
accompaniment, sang "Wapping Old Stairs."
It was some little time before she acceded to
her husband's wish for the rare old ballad.
Never before nor since heard I "Wapping Old
Stairs" sung with so much sympathetic taste
and sweetness. It was a pleasant sight to see
the kindly and admiring husband watching his
wife, and beating time with his unlighted pipe.
The elder Disraeli devoted some interesting
chapters to the matrimonial state of literature,

and the domestic relationships of public men is
an attractive theme, both with biographers and
readers. Mark Lemon's married life was one
of perfect peace and happiness. He married
early in life, influenced in his selection of Miss
Romer by the good old influence which in the
days of our grandfathers was not sneered at as
weakness, nor laughed at as sentiment. Love
matches in these modern days are the luxuries
of the poor; but even here education is necessary to make women understand their duties to
their husbands, and to develop the innate
chivalry of man, so as to keep him out of the
police dock for wife-beating. Not that Mark
Lemon was rich when he married. He had
his way to make; and with the aid of a loving
and devoted wife he made his way. Had he
been less anxious to do justice to his family in
the days of his prosperity, he would probably
have been less sanguine in the investment of
his earnings for their welfare, and more

successful at the last. The only home sorrow of Mark Lemon's life was owing to the comparative failure in the world of his eldest son, who, during a short career in India, suffered so seriously through change of climate, that for some years he had been disabled from any great physical or mental effort. This, however, was in a measure made up to the disappointed father by the unity and affection of his children at home; and latterly he was very much assisted in his *Punch* and other correspondence by his youngest son, Harry Lemon, who has written several dramas which are full of promise.

In the fields not far from Mark Lemon's pretty cottage at Crawley was a small farmhouse, where the editor of *Punch* wrote most of his latest works.

"I find it difficult," he said to me one day during a pleasant Sussex ramble, "I find it difficult settling down to work sometimes. It seems out of character, an old boy like me telling love stories."

"Experience gives old boys an advantage over young ones," I said.

"But the young fellows have enthusiasm and faith; for that matter I don't know that I have lost faith, nor sentiment either; but I hurry over love scenes as if I had no business with them."

"I don't think you do yourself justice. Where is your writing-box, as you call it?"

"Over yonder," he said, pointing to the outskirts of Crawley, "and I have spent some happy hours there. When one gets fairly started, scribbling after all is a pleasure."

"Truly. If authors are rarely rich in this world's goods, they have hours of happiness which riches cannot purchase.

> 'There is a pleasure in poetic pains
> Which none but poets know.'"

"It is a blessed dispensation, my boy," he said. "I hope I am not getting too old for its enjoyment. Writing does not come easy to me now. It often takes me an hour or two before I can work myself up to it. This is the process. A light breakfast or luncheon, and a steady walk to the little cottage-farm I told you of. When I get there I unlock my room, put out my paper, nib my pens, and get all in order. Then I go outside, light my pipe, wander into the farmyard, look at the cows, or the pigs, or the poultry, or anything else; sit on a gate, perhaps, if I can balance myself, sniff the local perfumes of hay and straw, and presently the fit comes on; down goes the pipe, up comes the pen, and away you go."

I know several men of letters who are in the habit of carrying their work about with them, in the hope of doing snatches at odd times. During the last five or six years Mark Lemon always had an unfinished novel in his bag.

He had chambers in London at 31, Bedford Street, where he wrote occasionally. If his bag was there you might be sure his unfinished novel was there also; if you saw the bag at his office in Bouverie Street, there you might be sure was his unfinished novel; if you encountered him in the train on his way home, there you would see his bag, and in it you might safely swear was his unfinished novel. You would be equally safe in saying that the story never grew at Bedford Street, nor at the *Punch* office. It was in that plain little room in the cottage-farm where the old man dreamed himself young again, until the failing brain and the tired hand brought him back to the sad Reality.

He may be said to have renewed his youth in Scotland during this pleasant tour of which I am writing. From the outset he had resolved that this journey should be one of pleasure. We had no cares, not only because we had no letters, but the entertainment was a financial success in Scotland before it began. The troup was engaged by the committee of the Glasgow Athenæum, and they were responsible for everything except stage management. Moreover, the Scotch showed a high appreciation of Mark Lemon, both as a man and an actor, and everything was conducive to happiness. There was but one hitch, and this was soon over. " I never had a happier time " was Mark Lemon's frequent comment on the day's doings.

On Thursday in that memorable week we left Edinburgh for Greenock, stopping on our way at the George Hotel, Glasgow, where the amateur impresario had duly ordered an early dinner. The Lemons had friends waiting to see them. Leaving them to take sweet counsel together, Shallow undertook to show me the house in which Bailie Nicol Jarvie lived. Shallow was, in truth, native and to

the manner born, and he was not at all pleased
with my remarks upon some of the incidents
which forced themselves upon our attention in
the neighbourhood of the Saltmarket. In less
than half an hour we saw two brutal fights,
one of which was terminated by the police,
only apparently in time to save the life of a
drunken rowdy without shoes or stockings.
Naked legs, more or less influenced in their
movements by whisky, were common enough
in this low quarter of the town, which had
given itself up to dried fish and whisky shops.
But the house of Rob Roy's Lowland cousin
seemed to hallow the Saltmarket, and make it
sacred ground. The Wizard's touch was upon
it. Where, indeed, is there a spot in all Scotland which is not sacred to the memory of Sir
Walter Scott?

It was in the locality of the Saltmarket that
we concocted a little pleasantry to accompany
the luncheon at the George. In one of those

miscellaneous shops which are to be found in the low quarters of our big towns, we saw a collection of the toy buckets which belong to children's parties at the seaside. Painted upon the outside, in particularly obstructive letters, were sundry Christian names.

" Have you a bucket with 'Harry' upon it ?" asked Shallow.

" Eh, mon, that have we," said the store-keeper.

" What is the price ?"

" Twopence."

" I will take it."

" How much for this figure of Punch ?" I asked.

" Saxpence," was the curt reply.

" Wrap one up for me."

In an adjacent shop there was a store of jewellery, such as would have paid a king's ransom, if golden glow and crystal glitter might denote intrinsic value. There were brooches, rings, bracelets, necklets, lockets, set with jewels of every hue.

"Here thou mayest lay out that thousand pounds which Falstaff will pay thee back anon, Master Shallow," I suggested, in Shallow's own vein.

"I know not how, unless I buy the entire shop," said Shallow, "and that may not be; but let us in, and see these Brummagem wares."

"'Tis well we buy some sweet trinket for Mistress Quickly."

"Aye marry, well said i' faith," Shallow replies.

A pair of ear-rings set with emeralds, a diamond ring, and a brooch of rubies and pearls, were our united purchases, and Shallow paid elevenpence for the whole of this magnificent collection.

"At dinner, during the courses, let these jewels and art treasures come in ready packed

and directed to the company, eh, Master Shallow ?   Gifts from admirers who saw them play,
eh, Master Shallow ?"

"Excellent, i' faith," responded Shallow.

"Thou art a man after mine own heart, Master Shallow, and wilt continue if thou'lt only
forswear long pipes and live in some fashion.
We have heard the chimes at midnight, Master
Shallow, *we* have seen merry times."

"That we have, that we have," Shallow re-
joined, always up in his part, "in faith, Sir
John, we have; our watchword was *Hem !*
boys ! Come, let's to dinner, come let's to
dinner.   O the days that we have seen !
Come, come."

And we "comed," as Artemus Ward would
say.

By the way, Shallow and Bardolph were
intimate friends of the deceased humourist, and
Shallow imitated the famous American's style
very successfully; so that occasionally we had

a strange admixture of Ward and Shakespeare. For example, in the Saltmarket,
Shallow having unintentionally run upon a
dram-drinker with the usual bare legs, said
dram-drinker offered to fight the amateur
actor. " No, my friend," said Shallow, "I am
not a fightist, but I can apologise;" and he
did, with mock professions of abject sorrow,
which the dram-drinker neither seemed to understand nor appreciate. "Hoot, mon, ye're
just daft I ken, its nae good hammering a
feuil." "By the mass no, i' faith," said Shallow, "you had better let me went." And thus
did he.

After the first course of our early dinner,
there arrived a mysterious but imposing looking parcel, directed to " H. L. Bardolph, from
an admirer who desires to give expression to
her pleasure by a little present." Shallow
crumbled his bread, and looked thoughtful.
Mistress Quickly was silent and anxious.

Bardolph seized a knife, and began to open the parcel. Falstaff commanded that the banquet should proceed. Bardolph, after much exercise of his knife and his patience, came upon the little tin bucket, inscribed "Harry," to his intense disgust and the general merriment.

"That's Shallow!" said Harry.

"What is?" was the response, "it is anything but shallow. On the contrary, it is a deep, roomy bucket."

"Thou honeysuckle villain," exclaims Bardolph, "thou Fustilarian, an I be not the death of thee I'm a poulterer's hare or a stock fish."

"Go to," says Falstaff, "here be other fish, aye and ready fried. Now, by my lady, this is a merry feast most sweet impresario."

And so it was. I call to mind few merrier. Ere the fish was removed there came in three separate parcels of jewellery for Mistress Quickly, "Real jewels," said the lady, "aye, she was sure of it;" and she carried the joke

6

further, to Shallow's annoyance, by wearing
the Brummagem trinkets with her Sunday
things on the "Sabbath ye ken." The feast
was concluded by the presentation of that little
figure of Punch which came from the Saltmarket, and Mark Lemon vowed it was an
excellent model, and one which he should
treasure.

"You remember that horse mounted with a
figure of Punch—it stands on my mantel-shelf
in Bouverie Street?"

"Yes."

"That was one of the figures in a grand procession modelled and sent from Germany years
ago, illustrating the imagniary installation of
Mr. Punch as a doctor of philosophy. There
is a diploma hanging by it in which Punch is
officially and legally set forth as Doctor Punch."

"Yes," said Bardolph, "the Scotch gentleman who made *that* joke, very much admired
the equestrian Punch. I shall never forget

that fellow. The governor, you know, very seldom uses anything from outsiders; not that he doesn't wish to do so, but because no good jokes come from outsiders. However, something, I forget what it was, came from Edinburgh; I think it made two lines; it was nothing particular. One day the author presented himself. You know how obliging the governor is. Well; he saw this gentleman from Scotland, who unfolded his business, which was to receive his money for the joke. The governor smiled, said he would see to it, and told the jokist to call the next day. Meanwhile he passed a little account for him for a guinea and left it with me. It was not worth a guinea, I remember the joke in question. *Punch* does not pay me on that liberal scale. I presented the memorandum to the gentleman when he called. 'A guinea,' he exclaimed. 'Hoot, mon, what gude is that? I've taen a week's holiday and come all the

way from Edinboro' on the faith o' the money
I'd get from ye.' It was true. How much he
expected I can't say, but he expected it would
pay for his week's holiday."

While we were talking some *bona fide* pre-
sents really did arrive. They were received with
great suspicion, but Bardolph's triumph was
complete when he found himself proprietor of a
handsome Scotch bonnet with silver mount-
ing and ostrich feather. Shallow received a
similar compliment, and soon afterwards these
distinguished members of the company donned
their new head-gear. There was some discussion about their right to wear the feathers, but
the authority was disposed of by the summary
process of ignoring it, and Bardolph declared
himself at once "a chieftain to the Highlands
bound." Shallow wrapped an imaginary plaid
about his shoulders, and defied criticism,
though he looked anything but dignified in his
bonnet. You need broad shoulders and a stal-

wart form to carry a full-sized Scotch bonnet
with dignity. Shallow was not " thiswise," as
he would have said, but otherwise, and he had
a cockney habit of sticking his hat on one side.
This is very laudable and characteristic perhaps
after an evening at Evans's, but a Scotch bonnet worn awry in the day time, and in Glasgow
too, does not add to the dignity of the wearer.

In due time we arrived at Greenock ; what
we could see of it by the dim light of gas, and
through the somewhat opaque atmosphere of a
Scotch mist, was anything but pleasant. The
Tontine, however, had a warm reception for us.

" This is a very nice bedroom—it will do
capitally," I said to the waiter who carried in
my rugs. He was a wiry, cunning, clever-
looking fellow, with something of the Flintwich
twist in his manner.

" Aye, it's all reight. Ye'll find everything
gude in this hoose," he said, unstrapping
my luggage. Then screwing his head round

at me, he added, "But ye'll hae to pay for it."

With which suggestive remark he left me.

My first desire in Greenock was to see a London paper. I found out a newsagent close by the hotel.

"Have you *The Times ?*"

The man looked at me vacantly.

"Or *The Standard ?*"

No reply.

"*The Telegraph ?*" I next suggested.

"*The Greenock Telegraph,* yes," said the man, handing me the local paper.

"No, I want a London daily."

"Ye'll get none in Greenock," he replied, with an air of triumph; "ye'll get nae London dailaies in Greenock: we dinna tak 'em."

On further inquiry, I found that *Punch* and *The Illustrated London News* were the only papers to be had in Greenock.

I encountered Shallow leaving a barber's shop.

"Been to get soap," he said, "always some-thing lost. The Prince is in a terrible way—just beginning to dress and no soap. Volun-teered to get some. Fine specimen of the native, the shopman. 'Are ye gaeing to see this Faelstoff?' he asks me. 'I am, sir,' says I. 'I'd like tae be gaeing mysel,' he replies thoughtfully; adding, as a finale, 'Aye, mon, there mun be summat in this Shakespeare, or he wouldna a lasted sae lang.'"

I accompanied Shallow to the hall, a fine building recently erected. The Prince was grateful to Shallow for the soap. Hal was most fastidious over his toilette. He made up the Prince admirably, looked every inch a Prince, though he confided to me, even in his regal habit, that he had had a splendid offer to go back into the tea-trade, and thought he should do it. This mixture of romance and trade, of worldly prospects and stage tinsel, struck me as peculiarly incongruous. Imagine

Prince Hal in the tea-trade. It would have
been far easier to regard my friend as a prince
indeed, than to have turned him into a commercial; for he was a fine, athletic gentleman,
with a bright eye and a commanding manner.
Presently I found him fencing with Poins,
who, in this tour, doubled that character with
the Chief Justice. Our porter was in great
trouble. Everything was all right, he said,
but he had lost his mate. He had barely confided his woes to me when his mate appeared.
His *mite* would have been a better term,
though the young gentleman was an important
member of the company. He stood about
three feet in his shoes, and played the page.
It was one of the most interesting scenes in
the entertainment which opened with Falstaff
and his page. "Sirrah, you giant, what says
the doctor?" Our porter (who, by the way,
used to "go on" as an apparitor) was
delighted to find that he had not lost his mite,

of whom he took quite a motherly care during our travels.

The play went off admirably. During his long "wait," Shallow had a serious conversation with my crooked friend the waiter, the result of which was the unearthing of as fine a bottle of port wine as could be desired. Falstaff pronounced it perfection.

"How old?" said the waiter afterwards, in reply to Bardolph. "How old, did ye say? Weel, this hoose has been in the trade ane hondred year, and I dinna ken when they laid this wine doon ye see."

Our actors' supper that night was a very pleasant entertainment; the comforts of a cozy fire and smoking dishes being enhanced by the pattering of the rain and the sighing of the wind without. Mr. Henry Johnston, the secretary of the Glasgow Athenæum, who had charge of the show on behalf of his committee, joined us, and Falstaff was in high spirits.

"This is a better supper than old —— used to give the actors at —— in my early days," he said by-and-by. "It was an actors' hostelrie, and once a week they had a tripe supper; the host, a humorous fellow in his way, presiding. Some of the actors got tired of this plain fare, and one of them suggested a change in the *menu.* 'By all means,' said the host, and at the following meeting the actors and a few friends were present, myself amongst the number. Ushered into the dining-room, there were great demonstrations of preparation. The host sat in state on a raised seat at the further end of the table; by his side stood a servitor holding a herald's trumpet. The table was thick with covered dishes. When we were all seated the herald blew a flourish, and the host in a loud voice said, 'Remove the covers, let the repast begin.' There were meats of all kinds, birds, chickens, game, tarts, fruits, everything we could think of; but they were the contents of a child's toy-box,—wooden meats, wooden birds, painted grapes, painted apples. A cry of disgust, mingled with shouts of laughter, grectcd this satire upon the actors' desire for luxuries. At the first burst of surprise, old —— in his loudest voice cried, 'Jem, bring in the tripe.' The wooden viands seemed to have whetted the general appetite, and we had a very jovial evening. It was the host's fancy to play the part of a king. At a certain hour the club broke up; the time of departure being proclaimed by the entrance of a page, who bore upon a velvet cushion a very large key, which he presented on his knees. 'Her Majesty, my Queen,' then said the host, addressing the actors, 'has graciously sent me the castle key. Farewell!' And so the club broke up."

Talking of actors, Falstaff told us how he and Leech had discovcred Robson acting in an out-of-the-way place where they had looked in,

having an eye to some particular bit of character. They were very much impressed with
the stranger's performance, and this, I believe,
led to his being engaged at a respectable
theatre in town. It was very rarely that Mark
Lemon spoke of his colleagues on *Punch* before
strangers, but the conversation this evening
turning upon something in which Shirley
Brooks's name was mentioned, he said, with
enthusiasm, " Shirley's is the most graceful
pen in London." Mark Lemon was peculiarly
unselfish in criticism. He seemed to delight
in discovering excellences in the works of
others. A naturally kind nature had been
influenced by the editorial watchfulness for
talent. He was continually on the look-out
for genius. If, however, he was slow to condemn, he was very emphatic and hearty where
he did condemn. His admiration of the elder
Kean, and his contempt for the younger as an
actor, stood out in remarkable contrast. But

Mark Lemon had stronger likes than dislikes. This moral balance was of immense benefit to *Punch* in the early days, when it was building up its reputation. Against anything like humbug he was a stout and persistent opponent. Spiritualism, for example, was a form of humbug which he detested. Just at the time when *Punch* was particularly fierce in its denunciations of spiritualism I had chambers in Bedford Street, on the same floor as Mark Lemon's rooms. One morning, before breakfast, Mr. Home, the apostle of spiritualism (and a very agreeable and pleasant gentleman, apart from his peculiar power, of which I know nothing), called upon me. He was in my room when Mark Lemon entered in his dressing-gown, anxious to give me some news which he had received that morning by letter. I felt myself in an " awkward fix." I did not introduce the gentlemen. They bowed to each other, Mark Lemon in his courtly genial fashion. After an awkward pause, Mark Lemon retired.

"Who was that polite and kind-looking old gentleman?" Home asked.

"Mark Lemon, the editor of *Punch*," I said.

"Good heavens!" exclaimed Home. "I could not have believed it."

Presently I breakfasted with Mark Lemon.

"Who is your friend?" he asked casually.

"What do you think of his appearance?" I asked.

"O, a decent fellow enough; why did you not introduce him?"

"It was Home, the Spiritualist," I said.

"Humph, can't compliment you on the society you keep. Lee takes an interest in spiritualism, he would like to know Home, I dare say. One of our fellows can do all those tricks of the table and the guitar business."

"*Punch* has been very hard upon Home," I said.

" If he likes to name a day and come to Bouverie Street, I will undertake to find him a fair and liberal committee; and, if we fail to see through his tricks, *Punch* shall recant. There !"

Death enhances in interest the sayings and doings of one who filled so important a place in the society of letters as Mark Lemon. It is often the more minute incidents in a man's life that are most indicative of character. The world is naturally and laudably curious to learn how its leading men carry themselves in daily life, and what they say and think behind the scenes of their public position. Terence advises the student to consult the lives of other men as he would a looking-glass, and from thence to fetch examples for his own imitation. In holding up the biographical mirror, it is a delicate and difficult duty to weigh what may be fairly considered private conversations and opinions. I have to thank my friends in the press for accepting these papers as discreet and entertaining so far. It is often the case that close and intimate acquaintance does not increase your esteem for a public man. His character is improved when you are left to fill up the portrait from imagination and by the help of his works. This was not so with Mark Lemon. To know him intimately was to esteem him the more; and it is in this nobility of character that lies the peculiar delicacy of telling his story. When it comes to be done from the beginning, his biographer will do well to make it a perfect history. "A life that is worth writing at all is worth writing minutely."

CHAPTER IV.

"HOMEWARD BOUND."

AFTER Greenock, a Saturday morning performance in Edinburgh was to close our visit to Scotland. If shaping our course homeward had not conjured up pleasant glimpses of our respective counties, Sussex and Worcestershire, I suspect we should both have regretted leaving the land o' cakes. As for the boys Bardolph and Shallow, the Prince and Poins, they thought about the parting with real sorrow. Let me except Poins. He had a wife. How soon Bardolph and Shallow might have followed suit in this respect, is a matter of speculation. Bardolph

7

had made desperate love to one of the prettiest
girls in Glasgow, but she had hardly recovered
from the shock of his "make up" in the entertainment, when the parting days came. "I
never saw such a dreadful man in all my days
as ye were," said the pretty girl when Bardolph presented himself after the play. "Why
did ye not tak' the part o' the Prince?" This
gave Bardolph a twinge of jealousy which
threatened the peace of His Royal Highness.
"I would hae liked ye better if ye had played
the Prince. Whatever did ye do to your
nose?" Bardolph's nose was an incessant
trouble. Nobody saw the actor for his nose.
If the part were criticised, the writer forgot
everything but the nose. On the stage and off
the stage, Bardolph's nose was girded at with a
savage delight. The hardest cut of all was the
pretty Scotch lassie's objection. I believe
Bardolph would have proposed for the young
lady's hand, but for this shadow which fell

upon their intercourse—this terrible shadow of " the burning lamp."

An incident of thrift closed my financial intercourse with Greenock. At an establishment that shall be nameless, presided over by a Scotch lady who shall not be mentioned, occurred the following conversation. Let me preface the dialogue by saying that the lady had in the course of business received a large sum from the Falstaff party.

Amateur Impresario.—I want to send fifty pounds to London, it is after bank hours. Here are fifty one-pound notes; will you give me your cheque for them?

Enterprising Financier in Petticoats.—Ye dinna ken one-pound notes in Angland?

A. I.—No, we have no paper money less than five pounds.

E. F. P.—And ye'll be wanting them changed do I onderstand.

A. I.—I can send your cheque to London by

post, for which I give you fifty pounds: you will have the benefit of the money for a few days.

E. F. P.—(Counting the notes.)   Will ye tak' a cheer? (unlocking her desk).

A. I.—One-pound notes make a man feel richer than he is.

E. F. P.—That's jest the only fault ye can find wi' em: I have felt it mysel' (filling up the cheque).

A. I.—I shall just catch the post, I think.

E. F. P.—Yes ye'll hae plenty o' time for the post.   It was fifty punds I think ye said? (hesitating).

A. I.—Yes.

E. F. P.—(Fidgetting with her pen.)   Hae ye got a penny?

A. I.—I think I have, yes.

E. F. P.—(Hesitating no longer.)   That'll mak' it reight.   It's better ye paid me for the stomp; it would look queer to fill the cheque up for forty-nine pund nineteen and eleven-pence.

Falstaff was amused at this incident, and advised that we laid it to heart for future guidance. "Thrift is the talisman of fortune, but we will e'en draw the line at the penny stamp," he said, "there is another matter, however, which is troubling me. Here is a telegram asking me to fix the dates for Bir-mingham, or rather to accept the dates men-tioned for Birmingham and Wolverhampton. I will not go to either place."

"Not go," I replied. "Why not?"

"I said at the outset that these towns and Ireland should be excluded from the tour."

"Well, it rests with you of course, but I think you are wrong. You can have no feeling against the people."

"Certainly not. I have no feeling against them; on the contrary. But I will not go, and there is an end of the business."

"Excuse me," I said, "you are making a great mistake. Sleep on it."

The next morning he fixed the dates for Birmingham and the neighbouring town, and we left Greenock for Glasgow. A few people came out to see Falstaff off, and we received the usual amount of kindness from the railway officials. Mr. Johnston told us a good story *en route.* There is a handsome public building close to the railway station at Paisley. It is the Paisley and Greenock Gaol. Before it was built the two towns fought for the privilege of possessing the gaol. A Paisley and Greenock man are travelling by train. They stop at Palsley. A stranger asks what that fine building is. The Greenock man replies, "It's jest the Paisley College ye ken." The Paisley man rejoins, "Yes, but we get all our students from Greenock."

Arrived at Glasgow we are received by the directors of the Athenæum, who proceed to

show us their famous city, commencing appro-
priately for luncheon, by a visit to Laing's, the
best and most complete establishment of its
kind in the kingdom. There are thirty different sandwiches, ham, beef, spiced egg, lob-
ster, crab, anchovy, salmon, potted meats, and
various other kinds that might puzzle Fin-bec
himself. Collops, cockalcekie, and other hot
dishes are here also, and drinks of every kind.
You help yourself as fancy or appetite dictates;
you draw your own wine, spirits, and beer,
pour out your own tea and coffee. No one
interferes with you. When you have finished
you go to the counter and rehearse your
luncheon, and pay according to your own
record. The proprietor has only on very rare
occasions suffered through the defective memory or morality of any of his customers.
The disgrace of a Glasgow merchant, who was
found defrauding the treasury, is a tradition
of the establishment. He was a rich man.

During many days he paid threepence for his
luncheon.   One morning an attendant noticed
that he consumed considerably more sandwiches and collops than would be covered
by this sum.   He was watched.   For a whole
week he was allowed to go on, paying his
modest threepence, or occasionally sixpence, for
luncheons amounting to five times that money.
At the end of this time his conduct was pub-
licly exposed by the proprietor before a crowd
of customers.   The merchant paid a large sum
of money to the funds of a local institution.
Being sent to Coventry by the commercial
community, he was, however, compelled to
leave Glasgow.

From Laing's we went over Messrs. Arthur
and Company's warehouse, which is said to
be the largest in the world.   We wandered
through labyrinths of shawls, long cloths,
linens ; we went upstairs and downstairs,
through tunnels beneath streets, now amidst

catacombs of cloth, now through rooms gay
with the picturesque plaids of Scotland.
Falstaff, "a good portly man, i' faith, and a
corpulent," struggled through this grand commercial tour with a zeal worthy of the highest
praise. Tired? No, he was not tired, he
said. He complimented the foremen of rooms,
talked about warp and weft, and freights, and
was as merry as man could be. From Arthur's
famous establishment to the ship-building yard
of Messrs. Napier was a pleasant drive. We
were most courteously received. The place
was bright with blazing forges, and noisy with
ringing hammers. There were tools of every
kind operating upon metal of every shape. The
ponderous planes doing work of rare delicacy,
the punching tools, and the steam hammer
with its elephantine capacity of power, excited
Mark Lemon's greatest interest. The perfor-
ating machine reminded him of a scheme which
he thought the *Times* might adopt. "Before

sending the paper to press let the sheets be
perforated on the same system as postage
stamps, so that they could be torn open without the use of a paper knife.   This would be a
great boon to railway travellers."   Messrs.
Napier had on the stocks an iron war-ship of
peculiar construction, which was being built
for Her Majesty's Government.

"Glad to see this kind of work going on,"
said Falstaff, "it is the only thing the Tories
are good for; they do try to keep up the fleet,
and after all that is our only national defence."

We next visited the Cathedral, a magnificent
church, built upon a commanding site, and full
of historic and archæological interest.   Murray
quotes a quaint Scotch description of it.   "A
brave kirk—nane of your whigmaleries, and
curliewurlies, and open steek hems about it; a
solid weel-jointed mason work, that will stand
as long as the world, keep hands and gun-
powther off it."   The crypt is full of strange

beauty, and has many peculiar and solemn associations. Thence to the necropolis was an appropriate and short walk. The University is close by. We saw the students in their red gowns, and were on the point of entering the building when Falstaff confessing himself tired, we adjourned to the " George."

' We had a fine house that night at the City Hall, a well-dressed house, gay with colour, and warm with life. Mr. David Masson was present, I believe, and many men of literary and dramatic taste. I noticed in the front seats a very solemn-looking gentleman, evidently "a minister ye ken." It was very soon apparent that he had mistaken the character of the entertainment. He came to see "readings in costume" and found himself in a playhouse. With an apparent effort he remained until the hostess entered; nay, he dared to witness that lively person go off in company with Falstaff. But at this point he triumphed

over Satan and fled from the evil place, no
doubt shaking the dust from his feet as he left
it.   An incident of this kind occurred at Chel-
tenham.   Mark Lemon used to speak of it
after dinner.   He had "stuck" in his part
twice through observing the unhappy gentleman, who rushed out while Bardolph was
telling the Prince how he had blushed at Falstaff's monstrous devices.   The Glasgow audience enjoyed the entertainment; they took
every point; and were even demonstrative in
their applause.   Miss Garland played Dame
Quickly with rare tact and spirit, and the
gentleman who during the Scotch tour doubled
Poins and the Chief Justice, forgot to talk of
Falstaff's "hoss," and was as lively and
spirited a Poins as he was judicial and dignified
in the part of the Chief Justice.   It was the
result of nervousness more than anything else
that made Poins invariably pronounce horse
"hoss," and lads "leds."   He knew when he

did it, and was duly laughed at behind the curtain, if not in front; it was one of those little verbal peculiarities which often require a great deal of practice and criticism to overcome.

In the evening the directors of the Athenæum waited upon us at the· " George " to say a few parting words, and to hand over a cheque representing the financial result of the tour. It was my intention to be quite garrulous about this meeting. I made notes of the rise and progress of the Athenæum; but the length to which these papers have already arrived, induces me to generalise the facts and figures of the committee's report by saying that the Institution is one of the best and most successful in the three kingdoms. The building is worthy of the association, the association is worthy of Glasgow. The enterprise of the committee in the way of lectures and entertainments is shown in their numerous and important engagements. In the case of our "show," for example, they paid for this luxury fifty pounds a night, I believe, and all the company's expenses. The latter were by no means trifling, and yet the committee made a very handsome profit for the Athenæum. They worked the business details of the engagement admirably. Their bill-posting and advertising generally was masterly in conception and execution. They never made a mistake. They combined, so far as their intercourse with Falstaff went, business capacity with kindly grace and courteous consideration. Upon the occasion of this farewell meeting some of the committee evidently expected Mark Lemon to be funny. There was a complete set of *Punch* in the "George" book-case, and the editor sat in the shadow of his own familiar volumes. He would surely sparkle and bubble over with wit in presence of such a mirth-provoking library. But Mark Lemon, like many other genial men, could

never be genial to order. He required time
for the development of his conversational
powers, time and perfect ease. My friends of
the Athenæum committee must have been a
little disappointed with their guest as a
humourist at this last meeting. One of the
gentlemen was unfortunate in a remark intended to be instructive and provocative of
talk. Just as Falstaff was inspired with the
happy thought of a pleasant anecdote, which
he had evidently caught wandering in his
memory, after a desperate search, a committee-
man spoke of the sanitary arrangements of
Glasgow. Now Mark Lemon had a hobby.
He was a director of a certain company which
is becoming celebrated for its manufacture of a
patent sanitary arrangement, founded upon a
sanitary law of the Israelites. The Glasgow
committee-man unwittingly led out Mark
Lemon's hobby-horse, and the Editor of *Punch*
mounted the favourite animal on the instant;

mounted it and rode it solemnly through an
Israelitish camp, through the Levitical laws,
through the government establishments of
India; mounted it and trotted it through the
camp at Wimbledon, gallopped it over the
Sussex meadows, and into the village of Crawley; finally pulling up, tired and sad, at
Bedford Street, Strand. That hobby-horse
was like a nightmare upon the meeting, which
closed solemnly with votes of thanks of the
deepest gravity. It is a dangerous thing to
plunge into conversation without a knowledge
of the hobbies of those whose tongues you
desire to loosen. Mark Lemon often laughed
afterwards at the Glasgow discussion on
sanitary science; but he always referred to the
northern city and the Athenæum committee in
words of pleasant and happy import.

I find it difficult to get away from Scotland, and yet fear to be tedious. I have
numerous suggestive notes lying before me.

Perhaps my best plan will be simply to let them lie before the reader also. Here they are, my closing memoranda of the tour in Scotland.

" Saturday morning .. to Edinburgh .. View of modern Athens from the railway station .. A stormy morning .. A few words on luck .. The only house in which Falstaff had a direct interest was that of Edinburgh, morning performance : it was the only poor house throughout the tour; did not pay expenses .. " Better to be born lucky than rich " .. Door-keeper had too much whisky .. Lost key of hall .: Back again at night to spend Sunday in Glasgow .. Bright, genial, appreciating Glasgow .. Cold, proud, classical Edinburgh .. Mem. for an article on the two cities .. The Broomielaw .. The river .. Within the memory of many persons when river at this point could be waded .. Energy of the Scotch .. Wonderful works on river .. A Scotch Sunday .. Land-

8

lord's pretty daughter said, in the sweetest
voice, with just a romantic suspicion of dialect,
'It would nae do to play the piano on the
Sabbath' .. No, but sacred music .. Would
not mind it, but the neighbours would hardly
think it right .. A Scotch dinner, sheep's head
(a splendid dish as done in Scotland) .. Cock-
aleckie (fine!) .. Mem.: To come to the
"George" another time, the very first opportunity .. Excellent port, i' faith .. A chat after
dinner, and a nap .. Sorry this is our last day
in bonnie Scotland .. Plots for plays .. Bardolph good at plots .. Our Prince a capital fellow, handsome, and carries a gorgeous rug
about with him .. One of the best-dressed
actors I know .. M. L. said a good thing: the
Prince 'doth give us bold advertisement,' is a
credit to the company .. S. winked at B.,
because M. L. did not like them to be gadding
about in those rakish Scotch bonnets .. Im-
portance of dress .. Scotch plaids .. Discussion

with Shallow about the clans .. Bardolph proposed the introduction of a good broad-sword
encounter, *à la* Rob Roy, in the Gadshill scene
.. Shallow to describe the tapestry after the
manner of Artemus Ward .. Tapestry as in the
days of Shakespeare .. Was Shakespeare part-
proprietor of the Globe Theatre? .. M. L. very
sorry could not inspect the cheap cooking
establishments for the working classes .. Athenæum directors gave some interesting particulars .. These establishments not successful
in London: why? .. Laing's would not do in
London: why? .. In the University a statue of
James Watt, and a model of Newcomen's
engine repaired by Watt: also a lightning
conductor over the cupola fixed by Benjamin
Franklin .. Mem.: Watt and Boulton? the
latter said to have been as great as Watt; the
firm at Birmingham was Boulton and Watt.
Boulton a plodder, encouraged Watt and

ʋ

forced him on.   Mark Lemon had this faculty,
always spurring others on.   M. calls on M. L.
'The *Times* has quoted my article from so and
so.'   'Indeed!' says M. L.   'Write at once to
the *Times*, and say you can furnish that class
of article to the *Times*.'   Happy thought!
M. did so, and was engaged .. Once M. L.
determined to give a musical composer a last
chance of reformation.   Wanted a libretto set
quickly.   Composer came—would sit up all
night and do it.   Mrs. L. objected, and the
more so when a bottle of gin was to be left
out.   Composer went to work: the L.'s went
to bed.   In the morning libretto untouched,
composer gone, ditto gin.   "Last time I saw
him," said M. L., "he had married the
Marchioness at a Strand cook-shop, and
his boots were black-leaded." .. We leave
Scotland in the morning (Monday) for New-
castle-on-Tyne. . This has been a green spot

in the desert .. Scotch thrifty, but generous, strong-backed, strong-brained people .. M. L. full of admiration of the northern character."

Monday morning was cold and wet, and we turned out from the "George" with real feelings of sorrow. We bought all the newspapers we could procure. One of the Glasgow critics took exception to the performance. The only unfavourable notice during the tour, it served to show up in bolder relief the criticism of the more appreciative journals. Arrived at Newcastle, we drove to the "Queen's Head," an old-fashioned hostelrie, not in the main street. We had hardly lunched before a waiter entered with somebody's compliments, to solicit Mark Lemon's autograph.

"Excuse me, sir," said the waiter, "it is just sixteen years ago since I came to you in this very room, and I believe with this same book, to ask you to put your name in it."

"Indeed," said Mark Lemon. "Sixteen years ago, is it?"

"Yes, when Mr. Dickens was here," the waiter replied.

"And you have not made your fortune yet?"

"No, sir, it's hard to make at waiting. Lady Don is in the house, in the very next room for that matter."

Mark Lemon visited her ladyship, whom he had known when she was a child. Lady Don was always a favourite at the Newcastle Theatre.

After the evening's performance Mr. Hare, the local agent who had engaged "the show," came in. He entered the room upon crutches. Falstaff inquired the nature of Mr. Hare's malady. "O, it's a long story that," said the local agent, "I had an accident, broke both my legs."

"Will you join us in a glass of whisky, our usual night-cap, and tell us the story?"

Mr. Hare, nothing loth, complied, and gave us the following remarkable narrative of his accident. I have headed it in my notes

"A STRANGE STORY.

"I had been staying at Tynemouth, and had to go to Cullercoats in the evening. I started to walk when it was growing dark. After I had gone a little distance on the road I saw a man walking in the same direction. It occurred to me that we might both be going to the same place. I said, 'Are you going to Cullercoats?'

"'Yes,' he said.

"'Which way are you going?' I asked.

"'I am going across the fields,' he said.

"I changed my steps to that direction, and then turned round to make some other remark. The man had gone. He had utterly disappeared. I could see him nowhere. I thought it very strange. It seemed as though

Fate had decreed that I should come to grief. I did not go across the fields. I suddenly changed my mind, and went along the road, why I cannot tell, unless the sudden disappearance of the man I had spoken to influenced me in some way. When I had gone along the road about a mile, this same man as suddenly re-appeared. He was at my side before I knew he had turned up again.

"'I thought you were going across the fields,' he said.

"I replied, 'So I am.'

"At my left hand there was a sort of bye-way, and the gate was open. I·thought that was the way across the fields. I entered the gate, and began to walk quickly, impelled by what strange influence I knew not. The next moment I found myself falling, falling, falling. I had stumbled into a pit. The thought came into my mind that I should never get to the bottom. Strange to say I fell upon my legs. The concussion was terrific; the light from my eyes seemed to show me where I was. I had fallen into a stone quarry about forty feet deep. I lay there for some time, and then called out for help; no help came. I had sufficient presence of mind to know that it would be unwise to waste my breath in bellowing. I might want all the breath I had. At intervals, after a very long time, I called 'Help! help! I have fallen into the quarry.' I lay there for hours. Towards the grey of the morning several men came and looked at me. I said, 'For God's sake, give me some water, I am dying—I have fallen down the quarry.' They gave a great horse laugh, and left me."

"The brutes!" exclaimed Mark Lemon, who was watching Mr. Hare with sympathetic interest, "The brutes!"

"I thought my time was come; I felt that I could not possibly recover," continued the local agent. "By-and-bye, however, some other people came round to me, found me out where I was lying; but they were afraid to touch me. I told them I would not hurt them, they need not be afraid. I had all my consciousness. I told them what to do, to get a shutter or a board and some water. I could hardly drink the water, not being able to move my head. I wetted my lips, and told them to lift my legs. At first they had no idea that both my legs were broken; I felt sure they were. Then I told them when they had lifted my legs not to lift my body, but just to push the board under me. I directed the whole of their movements, and they carried me to a wretched little public-house, where for some time they refused to take me in. Eventually they consented to my being placed in a smoking and drinking room. I was laid upon the table, and a doctor was sent for. It was found that I had broken both my legs and frac-

tured my back bone. The doctor said if the
men who had laughed at my cries and gone on
their way had come to me, I should have been
a dead man. They would have lifted me no
doubt, and if they had I should have died. I
had saved my own life by directing that my
body should not be lifted. I lay in this
wretched state at the public-house for six
weeks. I could not move my head. I had
lumps of ice, dipped in brandy and champagne,
put into my mouth. I had starch bandages on
my legs—the most terrible things you can possibly imagine. The pain and misery of starch
bandages is something terrific. As I gradually
grew better I told the doctor I must have
the bandages off. He said he could not
allow it; but finally he removed one. I
amused myself all night when he was gone by
cutting off the other with a knife, the pain
was unbearable. This occurred in August
last (1868), and this (February, 1869) is

my first appearance in public since the accident."

"A remarkable story—a wonderful story," said Falstaff; "very wonderful indeed."

"It is true, every word," said Mr. Hare; "and now I will say good night—it will not do for me to be out late."

Mark Lemon gave our visitor his crutches, and, walking gently by his side to the door, watched him down stairs.

CHAPTER V.

"OVER A SEA-COAL FIRE."

NOT with the brave old editor, not with the genial amateur actor, but alone in the firelight with memories that people the room strangely and sadly. Who could have dreamed when he talked of Falstaff's death that we should so soon be packing up our show for ever? Falstaff in his last hours babbled of green fields; Mark Lemon of old friends; of Leech, and Jerrold, and Hood, and Brooks. Not the faintest indication of the shadow that was coming made itself apparent in those northern days. We were too happy perhaps. One often pays dearly for being happy. It seems like a dream now, that northern tour, calling over the incidents as I do by the fire on this calm October night. The show is over, the actors are dispersed, never to meet again; here by my side is the leader's flask, yonder his text of Falstaff, there his letters, and here my rough notes of the closing days. The firelight flickers tenderly upon these sad memorials, and I call to mind other firesides and other times; firesides made merry by jest and fun; times made pleasant by friends whose chairs are empty, whose voices are heard no more. So close upon those last hours of that last journey, I feel inclined to repeat the experiment of my previous chapter, offering the reader a simple transcription of my rough notes, instead of any further modification or development of them. It is a liberty which I hope the reader will forgive :—

"Tuesday .. To Bradford .. The ride through the district in neighbourhood of Leeds; like a glimpse of Pandemonium .. In the evening a splendid house, but prices lower than M. L. had yet played to; was amazed when he saw the figures. Agent said Dickens could get no higher prices .. Tried it, and was obliged to issue large number of free passes .. Election petition just concluded; great excitement. Ripley said to have spent £30,000, his published election bill £7,000, and he has had to pay all the costs attending his competition for and against. A self-made man. Came into the Hall just as entertainment was commencing, and received a tremendous ovation .. M. L. had some friends in the green-room, old Bradford friends, who were excited about election affairs ...Promised to come again to Bradford .. Next day we all parted; Mark Lemon to London, myself to Worcester, Bardolph and Shallow to Birmingham .. Alone from Bradford to York .. Birmingham late on Wednesday night, determined to go to Worcester by the mail .. Found Bardolph and Shallow at the

Queen's.   Expected the real Impresario to
relieve me of the show here.   My amateur
labours at an end .. With Bardolph aud Shallow to see the sights of Birmingham.   Excellent theatre Simpson's .. Day's Music Hall,
one of the largest in England, the usual soften-
ing-of-the-brain kind of entertainment ; but the
management good.   Several fortunes have been
made here.   Mem. the degeneracy of modern
taste.   Better, nevertheless, that the working
man should spend his evenings here than in
merely 'soaking.'   No drunkenness allowed ;
children in arms not admitted, but girls of
thirteen and fourteen are taking their beer and
imbibing their morals with evident enjoyment
.. *Post* and *Gazette* have excellent preliminary
notices of Falstaff.

"Thursday .. 'Home again' at four o'clock,
and M. L. is once more at Crawley .. The
tour has been a success, but not made up for
the money lost at St. George's Hall .. At Gal-

lery of Illustrations, show paid a goodly weekly profit .. St. George's Hall (an unlucky house, though a fine handsome room for acting) was a heavy loss to the management .. Friday back to Birmingham. Good business there. M. L. much pleased with his reception .. Walter Maynard, the Impresario proper, in charge .. The Birmingham Market on Saturday. Everything to be bought here, from acid-drops to travelling bags, travelling bags to peacocks. A rare market—fish, flesh, fowl, sweets, vegetables, dogs, rabbits, boots, shoes, shawls, buckets, pickled onions. Walter Maynard entertained himself and a small crowd in the purchase of canaries and hedgehogs. Opportune appearance of Bardolph and Shallow. Delight of the ' Brums ' at Shallow's Artemus-witticisms .. Home at night, and write ' Finis ' to my first and last journey ' with a Show.' "

I fold up my notes in the firelight. They bring to mind the old familiar face, the genial

9

voice, the merry laugh. They carry me back
more particularly to a Sunday in May three or
four years ago. I spent the day with Mark
Lemon in Bedford Street. After breakfast we
sat over the fire and had a Sunday morning
chat. The sun came lazily in through the
venetian blinds. A cab now and then disappeared from the stand in front of the house.
The voices of children could be heard in the
adjacent court, and at intervals the sound of
the organ in the church where morning service
was being conducted. It was a quiet London
Sunday morning. The change from the cus-
tomary noise of the week, and the consciousness that business could not disturb him, gave
to Mark Lemon's chambers an atmosphere of
repose which was full of soothing calm. We
talked about a hundred wayside subjects. My
friend was in one of those dreamy fits of
looking back, which now and then gave a
special charm to his conversation. It was not

egotism which induced him to talk of himself
at these times, but the old man's delight in the
pleasures of memory. The young look for joys
in the future; the old have their happiness in
the past. Mark Lemon was happy in revisit-
ing his early days. On this quiet Sunday
morning his reminiscences were particularly
bright. I regret that this record of the day is
more an exercise of memory than a transcription of notes. Speaking of the plot of a new
story which I was then writing, and describing
to him how my hero ran away from home,
Mark Lemon was reminded of the history of
his grandfather, who left home when he was
a boy, because home was not as happy as it
might have been, owing to what he conceived
to be the unkindness of his father. " He
started off on the highway," said my friend, " to
walk he knew not whither. By-and-bye he grew
tired, and sat upon a gate to rest. A gentleman riding past pulled up and questioned

him, 'What are you doing there, my boy?'
'Nothing,' said my grandfather. 'Would you
like to do something?' 'Yes,' said my grandfather. 'Can you read and write?' 'Yes,'
said my grandfather. 'Can you ride?' 'Yes,'
said my grandfather. 'Then come with me,
and I'll give you something to do,' said the
gentleman. 'What is it?' asked my grandfather. 'Groom,' said the gentleman. 'No,'
thank you,' said my grandfather; for he had
been well brought up, and was accustomed to
ride his own horse. 'You have nothing to do,
you say?' 'No,' said my grandfather. 'Then
come along,' said the gentleman, kindly. My
grandfather went. Between my grandfather
and this gentleman, his master, there super-
vened the master's daughter. My grandfather
fell in love with her and married her. She died
in child-birth. My grandfather's father forgave
his running away, and left him a large sum of
money. This was his start in life. Many

years afterwards, during a single-stick match
at some village sports, my grandfather recognised in a sailor his own brother, who had run
away from home at the same time that he did."

Single-stick was common enough in Mark
Lemon's boyhood. "I belonged," he said,
in my early days, to the ancient fraternity of
St. George. I remember Master Betty. He
was a capital Friar Tuck at single-stick. They
talk of handsome salaries for actors now; why
Master Betty had fifty pounds a night before
he was thirteen years old." I think he said
he remembered Bartholomew fair. He remembered Richardson. "I was once presented by that famous showman with a free
admission to his booth. I don't think I
enjoyed it much. The play had a murder and
an accusing spirit in it."

Talking of the night-houses of London, he
spoke of "The Finish," in Covent Garden.
When this house was kept by Mrs. Butler, it

was a very celebrated establishment. Fox and Sheridan frequented it. But when Mark Lemon visited it he simply regarded the place as one of the curiosities of the night-side of London, which young men desired to see at least once in their lives. It was then a late rowdy house, the receptacle of the riff-raff of London after a night of debauchery. From "The Finish" to the prison is a natural step. Mark Lemon remembered the poor debtors of the Fleet Prison begging at a grating just as they did at the free prison of Ludgate, where Stephen Foster, who was Lord Mayor in 1454, won a rich widow while supplicating charity in this abject fashion.

Mark Lemon years ago edited *The Field*, and Leech drew some of the illustrations which then appeared in that well-known paper. He prepared the first Christmas supplement of the *Illustrated London News*, and for some years had a share in the management of the paper.

For a short time he edited *The Family Herald,*
and made such an earnest effort to give its
subscribers high-class reading, that he reduced
the circulation by many thousands a week.
One of the features which assisted to bring
about this result was the republication in its
pages of the "Waverley Novels." Almost
since its commencement he wrote each year
a Christmas story for *London Society.* He
was the author of forty plays and some
hundreds of ballads. Among his best known
dramatic pieces may be mentioned " Hearts are
Trumps," "The Silver Thimble," " Domestic
Economy," " M. P. for the Rotten Borough,"
" Bob Short," and " Gwynneth Vaughan."
His most humorous farces were " The School
for Tigers," " The Ladies' Club," and a
" Moving Tale." Some of his plays held the
stage very successfully, and " Hearts are
Trumps" might be revived with advantage in
the present day. Mrs. Stirling invariably

played Mark Lemon's leading parts. The Keeleys were very funny in "A Moving Tale." In one of those quaint little text-books of "Cumberland's British Theatre," with their clever criticisms by "D—— G——," I find "Honesty the Best Policy, adapted to the English Stage by Mark Lemon." The cast included Mr. W. Farren, Mr. Leigh Murray, Mr. Compton, Mr. H. Farren, Mrs. Stirling, Mrs. Compton, and Mrs. Leigh Murray. Mr. Lemon was in the height of his popularity then as a writer for the stage. "When we announce," says the critique introducing the play, "that Mr. Mark Lemon has adapted this drama from the French, it is a guarantee for its fidelity and also for its fun. The man who has made merry so many by his eccentricities in *Punch* could hardly fail to exhilarate an audience on the stage. Mr. Mark Lemon has also the happy faculty of drawing tears as well as provoking smiles." Some of the author's smaller pieces have been worked up into short stories, collected together in popular books, amongst which may be mentioned "The Christmas Hamper" and "Tom Moody's Tales." He wrote several successful books of fairy lore for children.

When the modern novel mania set in Mark Lemon was a veteran in letters, and it seemed late days to begin novel writing. But the prospect of increasing his fortune induced him to enter upon a new career, and he wrote "Wait for the End," in three volumes. This was followed by three other novels of equal length, "Loved and Lost," "Faulkner Lyle," and "Golden Fetters." Of these "Faulkner Lyle" is far the best work. While "Golden Fetters" is mere bookmaking, "Faulkner Lyle" is a work that any man might feel proud of having written. If Mark Lemon had been rich, these books would never have been produced. He might have struggled through one novel for the love of it—a novel in which he could have indulged in the narration of some of his own adventures, but he would have done no more. William Benton Clulow, in a work too little known, pertinently says "that competence of fortune and a mind at ease have in thousands of instances given the death blow to literary ambition and success." Men in the full and secure enjoyment of the elegances of private life are rarely found purchasing happiness by hard literary labour. Swift's works were the result of an ambitious desire for wealth and a title. Defoe wrote best when he was despoiled of position and means. Lord Bacon's most important works were chiefly composed during his exclusion from public employment; and Machiavelli wrote "The Prince" and "The Discourse on Livy" under similar circumstances. Mark Lemon was under no other pressure to write, however,

than the common pressure of the times, the
desire for advancement and competence. He
was in receipt from *Punch* of a salary larger
than had been paid to any other editor of a
weekly production, and he had other sources of
income. His last novel I have mentioned
previously. He called it "The Taffeta Petticoat." It is announced under the title of
"The Blue Petticoat." He had finished it
some months before he died. I have in my
possession his latest work, his last composition,
which has never yet been published. I pro-
pose to print it next month in the closing
paper of this series.

To return to that pleasant Sunday in May.
After our chat over the fire we walked down to
Waterloo Place, round by the Strand, and back
through Covent Garden to "The Garrick," my
companion pointing out houses of special
interest as the residences of celebrities, many
of whom he had known. "The Garrick" was

celebrated for its beef-steak pudding, to the
ingredients of which was added maccaroni.
He ordered this *specialité* and a claret cup,
over which we continued our wayside talk. It
was here that he spoke with almost the longing
of despair of two works which he hoped to
write. The first was "A History of *Punch*,"
and the second his "Personal Recollections of
London." The Falstaff entertainment had its
birth soon after this. When it was finally
settled that the scheme should be carried out,
Mark Lemon entered into the work of preparation with his accustomed energy. The
revision of the text occupied much thought
and attention, and after that the dresses and
engagement of the company necessary to support the chief. Mark Lemon's chambers in
Bedford Street were full of histrionic excitement for weeks. Falstaff was continually
entertaining not a score of tailors, but a host
of all kinds of theatrical people, costumiers,

agents, printers. In the midst of his trials of costume other matters would occasionally supervene to draw the actor's attention from the business immediately in hand. I see him now in his dressing-gown, slippers, and spectacles, poring over a letter at breakfast, having forgotten for the moment to remove from his head a tinpot-looking helmet which the costumier had brought for approval. It was a comical sight and amused the veteran immensely when he was asked to survey himself in the glass.

The dress rehearsal to which the leading men in London were invited, was an utter failure. Mark Lemon was nervous. Not an actor knew his part. They were all more or less influenced by the unmistakable nervousness of the leading man. It was a cold, critical audience too. The ordeal was tremendous, and Mark Lemon passed through it unhappily. It was not until he had got the

text well off by heart and his coadjutors understood his points, that the play went smoothly
and well.   Those gentlemen who saw Falstaff
on the first night did not see the literary actor,
who, being a fat man himself, had made a
special study of the famous fat man of the
great dramatist.   There were seasons in the
history of this Falstaff entertainment which
were gloomy and uncomfortable.   Now and
then Mark Lemon was physically unequal to
the occasion.   Any hitch in the management
or a bad house fidgetted and oppressed him.
Not an actor to the manner born, he was often
influenced by questions of detail which should
have been left entirely to others.   During the
first provincial tour he sustained a great shock.
Mr. Clarke, who had for years acted as his
secretary, and who did the duty of dresser,
besides walking on as an apparitor, was taken
seriously ill at Bath.   He died a few weeks
afterwards, leaving a painful blank in the little

company. Since then, within comparatively a few short months, what changes the great Scene-shifter has brought about in the life-drama of Whitefriars! The two commercial chiefs of the classic land behind Fleet Street, the founder of the *Punch* firm (Bradbury and Evans) and their editor and contributor of the golden days, have all made their exits and disappeared from the stage for ever. Three men who knew each other intimately in the early times of *Punch* died within a few months of each other—Mark Lemon first, then Charles Dickens, and last, Frederick Mullett Evans, who, with his late partner, undertook *Punch* when it was in difficulties, and who published the most important of Charles Dickens's works. The shadows come and go in the firelight. They make the quiet of a quiet room, with flickers of red and yellow on the picture-frames, seem almost oppressive, these shadows of past actors so recently in the flesh gathering amongst the more accustomed tenants of memory. How silently the great Scene-shifter works! He obeys no noisy signal. You cannot tell when he will begin to move in his everlasting drama. He needs no prompter. His scenes never hitch. He makes no mistakes, though we are sometimes tempted, like Tennyson's Farmer, to question the wisdom of His irrevocable decrees. He works by inscrutable laws. It is for us humbly to accept the inevitable, with a firm and lively faith in the mercy and wisdom of Him "whom time can never change."

CHAPTER VI.

THE LAST.

IT is many years ago since I struck up a brief epistolary acquaintance with Mark Lemon, though I met him for the first time in 1863. He came into the north of England to read "Hearts are Trumps," and was introduced to me by Tom D. Taylor, one of the most genial of west country journalists. I was living in the Bailey, at Durham, beneath the shadow of the Cathedral, and overlooking the river Wear. Mark Lemon accepted an invitation to stay with me here during his visit to Durham, Newcastle, and Sunderland. My house was a small old fashioned place. It had an ancient garden, full of old-fashioned flowers and old-fashioned ivy. At the end of the walled-in walks there was a terrace and summer-house, literally covered with luxurious creepers. From this vantage ground we overlooked the pleasant gardens of Mr. Wooler and Colonel Chayter, whose lawns and flower-beds sloped down in picturesque terraces, tier upon tier, to the very edge of the river. Coming from London to so quiet a spot, Mark Lemon was charmed with the beauty and repose of the place. In many letters afterwards he frequently referred to " that Paradise at the bottom of your garden." We smoked in the old summer-house and talked of London. There was with us on one of these days a ripe Shakespearian scholar, overflowing with literary enthusiasm, who had just completed a romantic play entitled "Passion and Parchment." It was full of poetic fancy, and in admirable blank verse. The gentleman to whom I allude is

well known in the north. I mean my old
friend, James Gregor Grant, author of " Rufus
the Red King," and several volumes of poems.
The son of an actor, Mr. Grant sat and
listened to Mark Lemon's talk of plays and
players with almost as much rapture as Pros-
pero's daughter experienced in listening to the
prince. The editor of *Punch* was like a mes-
senger from afar, coming into this out-of-
the-way city with news of the world. I see
them now, these two old men, the river rolling
by, and the rooks calling to each other. I see
the beaming face of the north countryman who
had not been in London for years, looking up
at the robust editor leaning upon the back of
a chair and making smoke-rings with a meer-
schaum pipe. On this same day we walked
to Finchale Abbey, and back again to the
cathedral. Mark Lemon was almost boyish in
his delight with all we saw and everything we
did. In these days I was editing the *Durham*

office was in Saddler Street, and again my windows overlooked the Wear. One morning when I was very busy Mark Lemon sat down and applied himself to some sub-editorial duties with great zest, saying, " I will be your sub-editor." He gave me ample proofs of his skill in this department; so that the Durham paper on this occasion had engaged upon it the most discreet and discriminating of London editors. Mark Lemon was every inch an editor, a director, an administrator, a nego- tiator, a diplomatist. He had the faculty of order and arrangement in editorial business, inspiring confidence among contributors and publishers. " I was made for *Punch,*" he said to me one day, "and *Punch* for me ; I should never have succeeded in any other way."

He came into the North to read, I said ; to read an adaptation of that very play the origin of which I have described in a previous chapter. He read at Durham, Newcastle, and Sunder-

but the reading at Sunderland was the most successful in every respect. He seemed to be on closer and warmer terms with the Sunderland people, than he was with the inhabitants of Newcastle. The interpolation of a line in the text put the Sunderland audience into a very excellent humour. I had recently told in print the following tradition of Sunderland, which just at this time was being much quoted by the press.

" A brusque but wealthy shipowner of Sunderland once entered the London office of Mr. Lindsay on business. ' Noo, is Lindsay in ?' inquired the Northern diamond in the rough. ' Sir?' exclaimed the clerk to whom the inquiry was addressed. ' Well, then, is *Mister* Lindsay in, see'st thou ?' ' He will be in shortly,' said the clerk. ' Will you wait ?' The Sunderland shipowner intimated that he would wait, and was ushered into an adjacent room, where a person was busily engaged in copying some statistics. Our Sunderland friend paced the room several times, and presently walking to the table where the other occupant of the room was seated, took careful note of the writer's doings. The copier looked up inquiringly, when the Northerner said, 'Thou writes a bonny hand, thou dost.' 'I am glad you think so,' was the reply. 'Ah, thou dost; thou macks thy figures weel; thou'rt just the chap I want.' 'Indeed,' said the Londoner. 'Yes, indeed,' said Sunderland. 'I'm a man of few words. Noo, if thou'lt come ower to canny aud Soonderland, thou see'st, I'll gie thee a hoondred and twenty pund a year—and that's a plum thou doesn't meet with every day in thy life, I reckon. Noo, then?' The Londoner thanked the admirer of his penmanship most gratefully, and intimated that he would like to consult Mr. Lindsay upon the subject. 'Ah, that's reet,' said our honest friend, 'that's reet; all fair

and above board with —— ; that's rect ;' and
in walked Mr. Lindsay, who cordially greeted
his Sunderland friend, after which the gentleman at the desk gravely rose and informed Mr.
Lindsay of the handsome appointment which
had been offered to him in the Sunderland
shipowner's office. ' Very well,' said Mr.
Lindsay ; ' I should be sorry to stand in your
way ; £120 is more than I can at present
afford to pay you in the department in which
you are at present placed. You will find my
friend —— a good and kind master ; and,
under the circumstances, I think the sooner
you know each other the better. Allow me,
therefore, Mr. ——, to introduce you to the
Right Hon. W. E. Gladstone, Her Majesty's
Chancellor of the Exchequer.' . . . . Mr.
Gladstone had been engaged in making a note
of some shipping returns for his budget. The
Sunderland shipowner, you may be sure, was
a little taken aback at first ; but he soon

recovered his self-possession, and enjoyed the joke quite as much as Mr. Gladstone did."

I had this from Mr. Grant, and published it first hand. It has had a long run since then, though it has not been so popular as the story of the collier pigeon fancier which I picked up some years ago in the neighbourhood of Ferry Hill, and ventured to quote in · a magazine article on "Pitman's Perils." Well, when Mark Lemon in his reading came to describe the dialect of his hero " Joe," instead of saying it was a very mixed kind of Yorkshire dialect, he said, in the best patois he could command, " It was nee like the talk of canny aud Soonderland." This produced a round of applause, and the scene in the kitchen, where Joe is hidden behind the roasting screen and thinks he will soon require basting, went down with a roar of laughter.

I thought of the difference between this reading and another which I heard at a fashionable house in Belgravia last year. It was a very aristocratic assembly. There was hardly any one present among the ladies below a duchess, except Miss Burdett Coutts. Several distinguished foreign artists were, however, mingled in the small group of distinguished gentlemen who came with the distinguished ladies. The walls were hung with paintings by the best modern painters, and there were " refreshments " which nobody touched. Mark Lemon had promised to read a scene from " Hearts are Trumps," and it appeared to me that, for once in his life at all events, he had not correctly gauged the taste of his audience. My friend was excessively nervous. He read the narrative of plebeian love-making anything but effectively. The ladies smiled with becoming propriety. The gentlemen applauded and said, " Brava," " Brava," " Excellent," in subdued and painful whispers. Indeed little was said or done during

the evening above a whisper, except when
Jules Benedict played in magnificent style his
own exquisite arrangement of " Where the
Bee Sucks." Later in the evening, or at an
assembly later in the season, Walter Maynard
entertained the distinguished guests with an
account of his experiences as an impresario,
and succeeded in keeping up a continual sim-
mer of amusement. The same stories told
from a platform and illustrated with songs and
music would prove a most attractive entertainment. When we (Mark Lemon and myself)
sat over a quiet supper at the Hummums in
Covent Garden, after the assembly had gone
home in its carriages or to another party in
the next square, we speculated upon what the
society of Vanity Fair would think of a history
of the strange and painful scenes that are being
enacted outside the Fair and on its very bor-
ders. For example, not far from the mild,
wealthy gathering at which we had assisted,

Jimmy Shaw was having a benefit night at his famous crib, where you may behold, in a glass case, stuffed (in the manner as he lived), the renowned dog Pincher, which had killed more rats than any other dog ever known to "the fancy" of any country, dying heroically at last, from blood poisoning, after killing some hundreds of sewer rats in the presence of an enthusiastic congregation of sportsmen and "gents" of position.

The Falstaff entertainment, as I have said before, was a failure at St. George's Hall. The public paid liberally to see Mark Lemon everywhere, except at this handsome but some- what unlucky house. There was, however, a serious difficulty continually in the way of the management. It was necessary that Mark Lemon should be in London two days a week. The claims of *Punch* exacted this amount of attention from the Editor at Whitefriars. These two days interfered with consecutive engagements for the country, and left a company idle during two and sometimes three nights out of six. Moreover, it is necessary, however excellent an entertainment may be, to " puff" and " push " it, and take every possible opportunity of bringing it before the public. The visit of the Prince and Princess of Wales and a distinguished suite to the Gallery of Illustration in the hands of a zealous advertising agent, might have made the fortune of the entertainment. Mark Lemon gave a special performance for the Court. The Gallery was decorated for the occasion, refreshments provided, and a special band engaged. At the last moment the manager found it impossible to be present, and but for Mr. German Reed, there would have been no one to receive His Royal Highness. Left to themselves, Mark Lemon and Bardolph had forgotten to have an attendant to take charge of the cloak room. In this dilemma the niece of one of the apparitors who was engaged in the property room was seized upon by Bardolph for the duty. The royal party had just entered. "Please to come this way," said Bardolph, taking the apparitor's niece by the arm. "There now, be very calm and quiet. Go into that room, and take off the Princess's shawl." With which startling command Bardolph quietly pushed the property girl into the room; and she proved to be quite equal to the occasion. At the close of the performance the Prince expressed a wish to see Mark Lemon, who came round to the front at once, and was of course graciously and kindly received. The Prince of Wales shook hands with him very cordially, and, on behalf of himself and the Princess, thanked him for the pleasure he had afforded them. The Princess laughed heartily at the scene where Falstaff assumes the part of Hal's father. The Garrick Club of the future may probably count among its interesting paintings a picture of Mark Lemon in his dressing-gown receiving the congratulations of the King (then Prince of Wales) and Queen upon his performance of Falstaff. The property girl pushed into the apartments of the Princess, and receiving her shawl, might make another interesting sketch. Painters of historical scenes have perpetuated many less worthy subjects than these two incidents of the modern representation of Falstaff.

A writer who knew Mark Lemon, and whose hand I recognise in the article, made my first paper in *The Gentleman's Magazine* the text of some interesting reminiscences in *The London Figaro*. Respecting the origin of *Punch*, he says Mark Lemon told him that he was not the only Lemon who flavoured the original bowl of *Punch*, for that there were two other Lemons associated with him—Leman Rede and Laman Blanchard. "Of course," my friend went on to say, "a little violence must be done to the pronunciation of 'L*a*man,' in order to bring it into harmony with the rest of the pun. 'Why was it called *Punch* ?' I asked him. 'Because the title was short and sweet,' he replied. 'And Punch is an English institution; everyone loves Punch, and will be drawn aside to listen to it. All our ideas connected with Punch are happy ones.' "

I once stood nearly half an hour with Mark Lemon looking at a Punch in Southampton Street. We stood in a doorway, and enjoyed the show immensely. Going to our rooms afterwards, he said, "What do you think my cabman had arranged for my especial honour?" One day in the week it was Mark Lemon's custom to visit the leading contributors to *Punch* in the way of business relating to copy and drawings. He employed each week the same cabman, who had bought a new Hansom for the editor's weekly rounds. "The cabby has built or bought a new

Hansom for me, and had arranged to have a
figure of Punch painted upon the panels. He
thought it best to speak to me before ordering
the work to be done, he said. I told him he
was quite right in his judgment as to the desir-
ability of consulting me; that I was much
pleased at his intended mark of attention in
the matter of the painting, but that I would
rather the cab were not embellished; that such
an advertisement was not to my taste. The
fellow to this day thinks I am a foolishly
modest and unassuming man in consequence.
I expect he would have liked to have done up
the Hansom in the style of a circus car. He
might have written upon it, 'Here you may see
the fat man!' "

This incident reminds me of a little episode
of the Scotch tour. All impresarios, of course,
wear fur coats. My friend of the Falstaff
entertainments, for whom I did duty in Scotland, generously insisted upon adding to my

"wraps" the impresario coat. It was a splendid seal-skin garment, somewhat too large for me. I wore occasionally a seal-skin travelling cap. One cold day, when Falstaff wished to take carriage exercise, I wore the skins in all their furry magnificence. Not alone doth manners make the man; the tailor has an important share in this human architecture. I was another man altogether in the new attire. During our ride I remembered that in one of my stories I had made a certain showman's chief wish consist in the possession of a fur coat, in which he hoped to strut about cracking a whip for the remainder of his days on the outside of an exhibition of natural history. When we left the carriage to make a call, the idea occurred to me. Dim remembrances of circus proprietors in painted vans came into my mind as I caught sight of my own short figure, very much disguised, in an Edinburgh shop-window.

11

"I don't like this coat, Mark," I said.

"Don't you? Not the impresario seal-skin?" said Falstaff, looking down ·upon me with evident amusement.

"No; I feel like a sort of agent in advance to a wild beast show or a circus," I said, gathering up some superfluous cloth, and wrapping the coat closer round my shoulders. "Do I look the character?"

Falstaff, with an air of mystery, glanced up the street and down the street, as if to be sure that nobody could overhear him, and then in a loud whisper, and with a hearty laugh, said, "Yes; by the lord, you do!"

This reminds me that when we arrived at Bradford we missed one of our rugs, and that in reply to a telegram to Newcastle concerning it, we were gravely informed that nothing had been left behind there but a small vessel with "Harry" painted upon it. This was the present which Bardolph received at Glasgow. We had another loss at Bradford. Mark Lemon mislaid a twenty-pound note. Search was made everywhere for the missing treasure, but it could not be found. I had burnt some papers, and it was shrewdly suspected that I had swept the note into the fire. By-and-bye, I found a sheet of note-paper with "Truly yours, Mark Lemon," written upon it in Falstaff's best manner. "Is this the autograph for the young lady who wrote to you this morning?" I asked. "Yes," was Falstaff's reply. "Then you have put the twenty-pound note into the envelope instead of your autograph." "Impossible!" said Falstaff. I rushed to the bar, and was just in time to examine the letters; and sure enough, as I had guessed, I found the note, much to Mark Lemon's chagrin, for he prided himself on his care and regularity in matters of business. What would the young lady have thought of Mark Lemon's reply had she received the other more marketable autograph which was so near being posted to her?

To return to my friend's article upon my first paper; he says he reminded Mark Lemon that the etymology of the word "Punch" would be perfectly carried out if its contributors were limited to five; for that "Punch" really meant five. Then they diverged into a talk on the old mysteries and miracle-plays, with the representation of Pontius Pilate and the Jews, and how there was a popular idea that the familiar words, Punch and Judy, were but a corruption of *Pontius cum Judæis*, and that the modern street-show of Punch is the only true relic of the mediæval miracle-play to be found in England. · Then my friend reminded Mark Lemon of the Sanscrit word for "five," which is *Pancha,* and the Persian, which is *Punj;* and how we are well acquainted with the latter word from the well-known Punjab or Punjaub, which in fact

means *Punj aube,* "the five rivers." "And, I
went on to say, that we derived our pleasant
beverage of Punch from India—or at any rate
from the East—where it was so called because
it was composed of five ingredients, of which
the Lemon was one.—I am aware that Dr.
Doran ascribes the origin of the word to a club
of Athenian wits; but I am unable to agree
with him in this particular."

They talked about punch of all kinds and of
particular pet drinks, but Mark Lemon did not
say what his favourite punch was. I think
his favourite mixture of this character was a
noyeau punch, for which a house in Fleet
Street is celebrated. But they did discuss
what should be the five ingredients that ought
to go to a perfect punch.

"We then talked of an acrostic charade that
I had shown him, on the words 'Lemon,
Punch;' which charade had, in fact, started

our conversation about *Punch*. It was as follows :—

THE LETTERS (5).

I brighten even the darkest scene—
I very nearly an ostrich had been—
I with a hood once pass'd all my days—
I am a fop in a play of all plays—
To its greatness the city of Bath I did raise.

THE WORDS.

I'm a Mark of judgment, of taste, and wit,
  O'er a crowd of pages I rule the roast ;
I mix with choice spirits, while choicer ones sit
  Around, while I give them full many a toast.
Of my two words, my first is squeez'd into my second,
Although at its head it is commonly reckoned.

The answers to the five letters were—Lamp, Emu, Marian, Osric, Nash ; the first and last letters in which words will spell the two words Lemon and Punch. Now, although double acrostic charades have been made so common, that they have been " done to death," yet at the time of which I am speaking they had not made any appearance in print. Who invented them, I do not know. In fact, in Latin, they are to be found in old monkish chronicles; but I am not aware who it was who first clothed them in their present modern dress. Before I spoke with Mark Lemon concerning them, I had seen them afford great amusement in private circles, and for six months or more had amused myself and others by writing them, receiving and interchanging manuscripts, and guessing or making the riddles. I submitted the above and other specimens to Mark Lemon, who, with his usual sagacity, saw that the double acrostic charades might be made generally popular. The result of our talk was that he asked me to prepare a paper on the subject for the *Illustrated London News*—with which newspaper he had then much to do. I did so, and it was printed in the *Illustrated London News*, August 30, 1856.'

This conversation closed with a joke of Jerrold's:—

"On that occasion I spoke to Mark Lemon of his tale, "The Heiress of Bilberry,' which had been re-published in the *Illustrated London News,* and which had been republished by Bradbury and Evans, with various other miscellanies, under the title of ' Prose and Verse.' 'Do you know what Douglas Jerrold called it?' said Mark Lemon, in his good-humoured, jovial way. ' He said that, as I was a Cockney, he supposed I pronounced the title "Prose and Worse." That was good, was it not?' ' It was characteristic of the speaker,' I replied, evasively."

The writer evidently interpreted Douglas Jerrold's fun into an intentional satire upon Mark Lemon's work. He did not know Jerrold as well as Mark Lemon knew him, or he would have accepted it in the Lemon spirit; for no man was more sensitive or less inclined

to hurt the feelings of a friend than Douglas
Jerrold. The humour of the Cockney phrase
suggested itself to the wit, and it bubbled up
to his lips. By the way, I mention in my
previous chapter the introductions written to
many of the little text-books, known as "Cumberland's British Theatre," signed D————.
G————. Although there is no doubt that
George Daniel was the author of these criticisms, it has often been suggested that they
should be collected and added to the works of
Douglas Jerrold. Quite as often has the question of their authorship been discussed and
"settled" in *Notes and Queries.* Blanchard Jerrold tells me that his father always
repudiated the authorship of these articles,
which were invariably headed "Remarks."
Even the author of "The Story of a
Father" and "Cakes and Ale" need not
have repudiated the work on the ground
of its want of merit. The opening of the

introduction to " Honesty the Best Policy "
is eminently trenchant and pithy; for example :—

" 'Honesty the best policy.'—Antediluvian
adage! Honesty!—ragged virtue, kicked out
of doors to beg or starve! He who now-a-days
ventures a word in favour of honesty, shall
be drummed out of society for a dolt and a
dreamer! The march of progression, in finding out a royal road to riches, has removed
this ancient stumbling-block. In the universal
scramble for money, nobody can find time, or
afford to be honest! Talk of physical malaria,
to which cholera is said to be first cousin ; look
at moral malaria! Metropolitan rank sewers,
quotha! What sewers so fœtid, what stand-
ing-pool so foul as the corruption that regales
the delicate nostrils of Capel Court? A stock-
jobber and a railway-director is a moral
pestilence that walketh not in darkness, but
that poisoneth in noonday. The noxious gas

of ten thousand carcases is not more destructive to the body, than the recking rascality of your living ones is to the soul; Yet this plague what shall stay? Not religion, for the God of the present day is gold. Not shame, the brass candlestick, like the schoolmaster, is abroad, and not expected home again! A Board of Health (when all are alike infected!) for cholera of the conscience—Ha! ha! ha!'"

This was written a good many years ago. Railway directors were in particularly bad odour when "Honesty the Best Policy" was produced. One of the most graceful impromptu compliments which Mark Lemon ever received was from a railway director. We were visiting the Worcester Porcelain Works, and had the good fortune to meet the chairman, Mr. A. C. Sherriff, M.P., a director of the Metropolitan Railway. Mr. Sherriff having asked me if I thought Mark Lemon would accept a memento of his visit, and, encouraged by my reply, begged him to accept a set of very handsome flower-vases which we had all admired. "Really," said Mark Lemon, withdrawing from the kindly offer, "I have no claim in any way upon your kindness." "Claim upon me," said Mr. Sherriff, "you have a claim upon all mankind." And so he had—all honour to his memory!

Mr. Benjamin Webster, of the Adelphi, was one of Mark Lemon's oldest friends. When the founder of *Punch* was a young man, hoping to win his spurs in dramatic literature, Mr. Webster was the first to encourage and assist his aspirations. I believe Mark Lemon's first play was produced upon the Adelphi stage. It is quite certain that some of his happiest hours were spent in the manager's room. As a rule he stayed in London several nights during the week. If he varied the monotony of Bedford Street by an evening walk, his footsteps were generally directed to the Adelphi Theatre.

He had a key to the manager's private door, the only key, I fancy, besides the one carried by Mr. Webster himself. How often he exercised this special privilege of admission *behind* behind-the-scenes Mr. Webster will remember now with painful particularity, since the last time of all has come and gone. If Mark Lemon had left Bedford Street in an evening without any message as to his whereabouts I invariably knew where to find him, and, thus meeting now and then at his favourite haunt, we finished the evening, after the play, in the manager's society. These were rare nights, when the men were talkative. They compared notes of past days, and gossipped of actors whose very existence had become almost traditionary: for Webster in his youth was intimately acquainted with an old playgoer who, as a boy, had seen Garrick. More than this, the manager knew an old man who knew a man who knew Cave, the founder of *The Gentleman's Magazine.* Mr. Webster knew Liston.

In one week in October last year Birmingham was peculiarly honoured. Charles Dickens, Mark Lemon, and Benjamin Webster appeared before large audiences of the Hardware Village. Charles Dickens inaugurated the session of the Midland Institute as the president of the year; Mark Lemon gave his "reading in costume" at the Assembly Rooms: and Benjamin Webster played *Robert Landry* at the Theatre Royal. It is a week which I shall long remember. I was favoured with a seat on the Town Hall platform, and never heard the great novelist speak more effectively. The hall was crowded with a host of Mr. Dickens's admirers. A noble instance himself of the triumph of industry and perseverance, Charles Dickens had to tell the meeting a no less remarkable story of the success of an institution which had long since taken to heart his

motto of " Courage, persevere." Not a word
which the president spoke was lost. He had
evidently prepared his address with particular
care. It was like a reading—*his* reading.
You could almost have fancied that he was
reciting an essay on progress. Every point
told, every sentence was perfect. He dwelt
with an air of wonder upon the great things
which the institution had accomplished. The
members of the institute listened with pardonable delight to the story of their own achieve-
ments. They must have experienced something
of the pleasure of the poet who hears for the
first time his own words set to the music of a
master composer. It must have been sweet,
indeed, to the early promoters of the association to hear the story of their triumphs set to
the music of Charles Dickens's noble words.
At the close of the evening he referred to his
resumption of the labours of his earlier years,
and promised his midland friends at an early

day the first instalment of "Edwin Drood."
I saw him the next day for the last time. He
was looking at the pictures in the window of
the *Illustrated Midland News*. In the evening
from the wing of the Birmingham Theatre I
saw Webster wipe the tears from his eyes after
that most touching scene between father and
child which lifts the " Willow Copse " out of
the common category of ordinary melodramas.
The next night there was what we used to call
during our northern tour an actors' supper at
the Great Western Hotel, with Mark Lemon
and Webster among the guests. Time has but
marked twelve months since then, and the professional brother writes to me thus of the two
famous amateurs: "I miss poor dear Mark
greatly. His loss and that of Charles Dickens
grieved me sadly. I can scarcely realise that
they are dead."

Speaking of Birmingham, it is interesting to
know that when Mr. Webster as a boy had

resolved upon adopting the stage as a profession, he went to Birmingham to seek an engagement. It was here that he purchased his first piece of theatrical property—a sword which he intended to use as *Rolla*. As a youth, it was his ambition to play this part. It is a curious fact that throughout his long and varied career he has never played the part for which he purchased the Birmingham weapon. I thought it a singular coincidence that an incident in Mr. Webster's career should have been identical with the first adventure of "Christopher Kenrick." The hero of the fiction ran away from home, and was pushed by adverse circumstances into the position of second fiddle in an orchestra. "I ran away," said Webster, "bought a sword to play *Rolla*, and became second fiddle in the orchestra."

There was with us during this evening at Birmingham, and on other occasions, the impresario proper of "Falstaff." I have mentioned him

12

previously under his *nom de plume* of "Walter
Maynard." The son of the late Mr. Beale, of
the well-known firm of Cramer, Beale, & Co.,
Walter Maynard is better known to a large
circle of friends as Willert Beale. Lord
Carlisle paid him the compliment of saying
that he reminded him of Tom Moore, Mr.
Beale having written many charming songs,
which he sings to his own graceful pianoforte
accompaniments. Longfellow's mournfully tender and musical words have never been more
sympathetically set than in Walter Maynard's
versions of "The Children," "A Rainy Day,"
and "Under the Lindens." The author of a
bright, chatty book entitled "The Enterprising
Impressario;" he has contributed some interesting articles on music to *The Gentleman's
Magazine,* and other publications. He had
arranged with Mark Lemon for the joint publication of six original songs. The following
was to begin the series :—

"A WAYWARD WOMAN."

"My coat is worn threadbare and thin,
    My shoes are very old,
The wind and snow alike creep in,
    And bite me with their cold.

"I've not a penny in my purse,
    Nor friend to give, not I ;
And yet my fortunes might be worse :
    Here are the reasons why.

"I might have been p'rhaps fool enough
    To give my heart away,
And met with coldness and rebuff,
    As men do every day.

"A wayward woman is a curse,
    You'll find so if you try¡
My state, you see, might have been worse
    And here's good reason why.

"I might have found a faithless friend,
    To change my sweetheart's mind :
Falsehood like this, you may depend,
    Is worse than wintry wind.

"Though to good cheer I'm not averse,
    Yet I can pass it by,
And feel my state might have been worse—
    You've heard the reasons why."

A WAYWARD WOMAN.

Words by the Late MARK LEMON.   Music by WALTER MAYNARD.

Con vigore.

My   coat   is worn thread

bare and thin, My shoes are ve - ry   old,   The wind and snow a -

like creep in, And bite me with their cold,   I've not a penny

in my purse, nor friend to give not I,   And yet,   my

for - tunes might   be worse, There is,   There

is   good rea - son   why,   I

Vivace Semplice.

might have been perhaps fool e - nough, To give my heart a -
might have found a faithless friend, To change my sweetheart's

way,   And met with cold-ness or re - buff as
mind,   And she   a will - ing ear might lend, To

men do ev - ry day, A wayward wo-man is a
false-hood most un - kind, To charming girls i'm not a

curse, You'll find so if you try, A
- verse, Tho' oft they make me sigh, But a

wayward woman is a curse, You'll find so if you

rall. parlante.

try, my state you see might have been worse and

rall - en - tan - do. *molto.*

f *p* *f cres.*

there's good reason, with a wayward woman, & there's good reason

cres....................................cen..............

p *rall.*

with a way-ward wo-man, My state you see might have been

..................do.

worse,   there is   good   rea - son why.
you know the   rea - son why.

1st. time. | Last time.

I. why

Dal segno.

The following is Mark Lemon's last complete song. I have before me a rough sketch of what was intended to be the second of the series, and it is in truth Mark Lemon's very last writing in this branch of composition. It is written in pencil on a sheet of blue-wove foolscap paper. There is no title to the design. The words are as follows :—

> " We are two heroes come from strife :
>   Where have we been fighting ?
> On the battle-field of life,
>   Doing wrong, wrong righting.
>
> " Forth we went a gallant band—
>   Youth, Love, Gold, and Pleasure ,
> Who, we said, can us withstand ?
>   Who dare lances measure ?
>
> " Round about the world we went ;
>   'Ne'er were such free lances
> Victors, in each tournament
>   Winning beauty's glances.
>
> " Gold at last his prowess lost,
>   And when he departed
> Pleasure's lance was rarely crossed,
>   Pleasure grew faint-hearted."

A few words in conclusion about Mark Lemon as the Christmas contributor of *London Society*. For many years past he occupied the foremost place in the Christmas number of that periodical. As long as I knew him he always had a short story in hand for *London Society*. It frequently happened that he did this work in the summer. I found him one summer evening in Bedford Street (with all the windows open, and letting in the sultry vegetable air of Covent Garden) engaged upon a Christmas story.

"I am glad you are come," he said, taking off his spectacles. "The Muse is a halting faggot to-night; I can do nothing with her."

"What are your intentions with regard to her ladyship?" I asked.

"I have been trying to induce her to help me with a Christmas story for *London Society*. They like the copy early, and I always try to let them have it."

"Better finish it at Crawley," I suggested.

"It is harder work to cover the fields with snow there than to think of winter here," was his reply. "Let us brew a cup, and then go and see Webster."

I suspect the "Punch" dinners set the fashion of "cups" among the "Punch" men. More than one of the fraternity is excellent at brewing summer drinks. The late Charles Dickens prided himself upon a mixture which was known as the "cider cup of Gad's Hill." It was made of cider, limes, pine-apple, toasted apples, lemon peel, and sugar, just dashed with brandy. The cup which Mark Lemon and myself compounded in the midst of the *London Society* story was a claret cup. The ingredients were simply claret, soda-water, lemon, sugar, a teaspoonful of brandy, and some ice.

"If we cannot conjure up snow for *London Society* we can conjure up ice for our cup," said Mark, stirring round the jorum with a spoon. "Claret-cup is your only liquor; my love to you!"

It did one good to see the fine old editor quaff the summer beverage. Whatever he did, he did heartily, reading, writing, eating, drinking. His likes and dislikes were equally ardent and energetic. He worked with all his might.

When Sylvanus Urban laid aside his lace ruffles and buckled shoes and came forth as a modern English gentleman, the new series of *The Gentleman's Magazine* was inaugurated by a dinner at the Crystal Palace. The then publishers invited the Whitefriars staff to the feast, and Mark Lemon sat on the right hand of the chair. None of that famous company enjoyed themselves more heartily than Mark Lemon. Even his witty contributor, Mr. Burnand, could not keep pace with the editor's jokes and repartee. When the time for speaking came, Mr. Evans (who, like his old friend Mark, has

now gone to his rest) in pleasant banter told
how Mark Lemon and Douglas Jerrold brought
"Punch" to his firm.   Mark Lemon was
earnest and happy in responding to the toast of
his health.   At night he took to the fireworks
with almost boyish delight, crying, "Oh!"
with affected wonder at the rockets, and com-
paring notes with his friend, Shirley Brooks,
about the pyrotechnic displays of Vauxhall.
It was "Punch" that named Sir Joseph Paxton's building the Crystal Palace.   Mr.
Punch's young men have always been lavish
in their praises of that establishment.   Sir
Joseph, I believe, was among the few outsiders
admitted to the "Punch" dinners.   There was
an intimate friendship between Mark Lemon
and the duke's famous agent.   Indeed, the
Duke of Devonshire himself was on familiar
and friendly terms with the leading members of
the "Punch" staff.   Mark Lemon's visits to
Chatsworth were among his sunniest memories.

Mr. Horne, who has just returned to England after seventeen years' absence abroad, is writing a work on " Bygone Celebrities," and will, no doubt, give us some interesting reminiscences of the early days of the Guild of Literature and Art.

I remember when a boy walking through Chatsworth Park, with a girl who accepted me as her husband soon afterwards, and meeting the duke, who was indulging in a quiet excursion through his own grounds. It was a holiday time in summer. The sun was flashing upon the gilded casements of the palace. Happy throngs of pleasure-seekers were rambling about the park and in and out of the house. Among the crowd I noticed a Bath chair occupied by an elderly gentleman in a white hat. He was watching the various groups of holiday people evidently unknown to anyone, a stranger to the crowd that was enjoying his hospitality.

my hat.   He returned my salute with avidity,
and looked almost grateful for the stranger's
recognition.   He turned round to watch us as
we disappeared behind the magnificent trees
which make such soothing shadows on the grass
of the most beautiful park in the world.   Soon
afterwards the Duke's chair was empty, and
the old man had passed away for ever.   Mark
Lemon was reminded of many excellent traits in
the Duke's character when I told him this little
story, and he was also warm in his praise of Sir
Joseph Paxton, whose house and grounds in
Chatsworth Park had all the luxurious glow of
the Duke's own place.   Two years ago I had
the pleasure of entertaining Mark Lemon and
a few friends at Worcester.   There were some
excellent people present, including a gentleman of position in the North of England,
accustomed to "the highest and the best society."   The conversation turning upon royalty,
my distinguished friend from the north spoke

of a rubber which he had played with the Prince and Princess of Teck.

"That completely floored me," said Mark Lemon, afterwards. "When I am in big society I can play off a duke as my friend; but I generally lead up to him through a bishop. The duke is my last card, my ace of trumps; but our friend from the north leading off with a princess I had no opportunity of airing my ducal friendship."

They were glorious days those days at Chatsworth for the hard-worked literary men of London. The palace with its gilded windows, the green park with its grand old trees, the silvery Derwent wandering through the flowery meadows; the luxury, the freedom, the splendour of the ducal house—so great a change from the noise and bustle and din and dirt of London—must have added brighter hues now and then to the inspiration of the guests.

"It was also a delightful time, I can assure

13

you, in town, at Devonshire House," said Mr.
Horne, the other day, looking back along the
path of his memory, as if he were checking
off the landmarks by the way. "I am afraid
to say how many rehearsals we had there for
the play—a dozen at least—and upon each
occasion the grandest, the most superb *déjeu-
ner*. The Duke was a gentleman in manner
and feeling. Some of us arrived at the house
in anything but brilliant equipages. We did
not all drive our own carriages, you know.
But in whatever manner we came, the gates
flew open like the gates of some magician's
palace in the Arabian Nights, and care halted
behind us."

Mark Lemon often spoke of his visits to
Chatsworth; as he did also of the election at
Boston, when his friend Herbert Ingram, of
the *Illustrated London News*, was elected.

"I was never a speaker, as you know;
but I held forth at one or two small meetings,

and the greatest hit I made was when I asked them who gave to Boston the practical blessings of water. Ingram had done something to get the Act for supplying the town with water, and this reference to his success told immensely."

Mark Lemon's Christmas stories may be taken as the key to his generous, self-denying, and loving nature. They are simple, unpretentious contributions to the literature of fiction, full of tender, gentle feeling, teeming with sympathy for artists, overflowing with a genuine and honest love for the drama and its surroundings, and abounding with sympathy for " the fatherless children and widows, and all that are desolate and oppressed." Mark Lemon entered heart and soul into the festivities of Christmas, and among his children was a child himself in presence of the holly and the mistletoe. In many a Christmas cartoon, in many a genial, merry, honest face intended to represent " Father Christmas," may be traced

the lineaments of Mark Lemon's well-known
features.   At Crawley it will seem as if " Father
Christmas " himself were dead indeed, now that
the snow lies white and cold upon the grave of
him who was everybody's adviser and friend in
the little Sussex village.

THE STORY

OF

FALSTAFF,

SELECTED FROM KING HENRY IV.,

FOR

DRAWING-ROOM REPRESENTATION.

BY

MARK LEMON.

SELECTED SCENES

FROM

KING HENRY THE FOURTH.

PART I.

SCENE I.—AN APARTMENT BELONGING TO THE PRINCE OF WALES.

PRINCE OF WALES *and* SIR JOHN FALSTAFF.

Fal. Now, Hal, what time of day is it, lad?

Prince. Thou art so fat-witted, with drinking of old sack, and unbuttoning thee after supper, and sleeping upon benches after noon, that thou hast forgotten to demand that truly, which thou wouldst truly know. What a devil hast thou to do with the time of the day? unless hours were cups of sack, and minutes capons, I see no reason why thou shouldst be so superfluous, to demand the time of the day.

Fal. Indeed, you come near me now, Hal; for we that take purses, go by the moon and seven stars, and not by Phœbus—he, "that wand'ring knight so fair." And, I pray thee, sweet wag, when thou art king—as heav'n save thy grace, (majesty, I should say; for grace thou wilt have none)——

Prince. What! none?

Fal. No, by my troth; not so much as will serve to be a prologue to an egg and butter.

Prince. Well, how then? come, roundly, roundly.

Fal. Marry, then, sweet wag, when thou art king, let not us, that are 'squires of the night's body, be called thieves of the day's beauty; let us be—Diana's foresters, gentlemen of the shade, minions of the moon: and let men say, we be men of good government; being governed, as the sea is, by our noble and chaste mistress, the moon, under whose countenance we steal.

Prince.—Thou sayest well; and it holds well too: for the fortune of us that are the moon's men, doth ebb and flow like the sea; being governed, as the sea is, by the moon. As, for proof, now: a purse of gold most resolutely snatched on Monday night, and most dissolutely spent on Tuesday morning; got with swearing—"lay by;" and spent with crying—"bring in:" now, in as low an ebb as the foot of the ladder, and by and by, in as high a flow as the ridge of the gallows.

Fal. Thou say'st true, lad. And is not my hostess of the tavern a most sweet wench?

Prince. As the honey of Hybla, my old lad of the castle. And is not a buff jerkin a most sweet robe of durance?

Fal. How now, how now, mad wag? What, in thy quips and thy quiddities? What a plague have I to do with a buff jerkin?

Prince. Why, what a plague have I to do with my hostess of the tavern?

Fal. Well, thou hast called her to a reckoning many a time and oft.

Prince. Did I ever call for thee to pay thy part?

Fal. No; I'll give thee thy due: thou hast paid all there.

Prince. Yea, and elsewhere, so far as my coin would stretch: and, where it would not, I have used my credit.

Fal. Yea, and so used it, that, were it not here apparent that thou art heir apparent,— But I pr'ythee, sweet wag, shall there be gallows standing in England when thou art king? and resolution thus fobbed as it is, with the rusty curb of old father antic—the law? Do not thou, when thou art king, hang a thief.

Prince. No; thou shalt.

Fal. Shall I? O rare! I'll be a brave judge.

Prince. Thou judgest false already; I mean, thou shalt have the hanging of the thieves, and so become a rare hangman.

Fal. Well, Hal, well; and in some sort it jumps with my humour, as well as waiting in the court, I can tell you.

Prince. For obtaining of suits?

Fal. Yea, for obtaining of suits; whereof the hangman hath no lean wardrobe. 'Sblood, I am as melancholy as a gib-cat, or a lugged bear.

Prince. Or an old lion, or a lover's lute.

Fal. Yea, or the drone of a Lincolnshire bagpipe.

Prince. What say'st thou to a hare, or the melancholy of Moor-ditch?

Fal. Thou hast the most unsavoury similes; and art, indeed, the most comparative, rascallest—sweet young prince—but, Hal, I pr'ythee trouble me no more with vanity. I would to heaven thou and I knew where a commodity of good names were to be bought. An old lord of the council rated me the other day in the street about you, sir; but I marked him not :

and yet he talked very wisely; but I regarded him not: and yet he talked wisely, and in the street too.

Prince. Thou didst well; for wisdom cries out in the streets, and no man regards it.

Fal. O, thou hast abominable iteration; and art, indeed, able to corrupt a saint. Thou hast done much harm upon me, Hal—Heav'n forgive thee for it! Before I knew thee, Hal, I knew nothing; and now am I, if a man should speak truly, little better than one of the wicked. I must give over this life, and I will give it over; an' I do not I am a villain.

Prince. Where shall we take a purse to-morrow, Jack?

Fal. Where thou wilt, lad; I'll make one; an' I do not, call me villain, and baffle me.

Prince. I see a good amendment of life in thee; from praying to purse-taking.

Fal. Why, Hal, 'tis my vocation, Hal; 'tis no sin for a man to labour in his vocation.

Enter POINS.

Prince. Good-morrow, Ned.

Poins. Good-morrow, sweet Hal. What says Monsieur Remorse? · What says Sir John Sack-and-sugar? But, my lads, my lads, to-morrow morning, by four o'clock, early at Gadshill—there are pilgrims going to Canterbury with rich offerings, and traders riding to London with fat purses: I have visards for you all, you have horses for yourselves: Gadshill lies to-night in Rochester: I have bespoke supper in Eastcheap: we may do it as secure as sleep. If you will go, I will stuff your purses full of crowns; if you will not, tarry at home, and be hanged.

Fal. Hear ye, Yedward; if I tarry at home, and go not, I'll hang you for going.

Poins. You will, chops?

Fal. Hal, wilt thou make one?

Prince. Who! I rob? I a thief? Not I, by my faith.

Fal. There's neither honesty, manhood, nor good fellowship in thee; nor thou camest not of the blood-royal, if thou darest not stand for ten shillings.

Prince. Well, then, once in my days I'll be a mad cap!

Fal. Why, that's well said.

Prince. Well, come what will, I'll tarry at home.

Fal. I'll be a traitor then, when thou art king.

Prince. I care not.

Poins. Sir John, I pr'ythee, leave the prince and me alone; I will lay him down such reasons for this adventure, that he shall go.

Fal. Well, may'st thou have the spirit of persuasion, and he the ears of profiting; that what thou speakest may move, and what he hears may be believed; that the true prince may (for recreation sake) prove a false thief; for the poor abuses of the time want counte-

nance. Farewell: you shall find me in Eastcheap. [*Exit* FALSTAFF.

Prince. Farewell, thou latter spring! farewell, Allhallown summer!

Poins. Now, my good sweet honey-lord, ride
with us to-morrow; I have a jest to execute,
that I cannot manage alone. Falstaff, Bardolph, Peto, and Gadshill shall rob those men
that we have already waylaid; yourself and I
will not be there: and, when they have the
booty, if you and I do not rob them, cut this
head from my shoulders.

Prince. But how shall we part with them in
setting forth?

Poins. Why, we will set forth before, or
after them, and appoint them a place of meeting, wherein it is at our pleasure to fail; and
then will they adventure upon the exploit
themselves: which they shall have no sooner
achieved, but we'll set upon them.

Prince. Ay, but 'tis like, that they will

know us, by our horses, by our habits, and by every other appointment, to be ourselves.

Poins. Tut! our horses they shall not see, I'll tie them in the wood; our visards we will change, after we leave them; and I have cases of buckram, for the nonce, to immask our noted outward garments.

Prince. But I doubt, they will be too hard for us.

Poins. Well, for two of them, I know them to be as true-bred cowards as ever turned back; and for the third, if he fight longer than he sees reason, I'll forswear arms. The virtue of this jest will be, the incomprehensible lies that this same fat rogue will tell us, when we meet at supper; how thirty, at least, he fought with; what wards, what blows, what extremities he endured; and in the reproof of this lies the jest.

Prince. Well, I'll go with thee: provide us

all things necessary, and meet me to-morrow
night in Eastcheap, there I'll sup : farewell.

Poins. Farewell, my lord.   [*Exit.*

Prince. I know you all, and will awhile up-
hold

The unyok'd humour of your idleness :

Yet herein will I imitate the sun ;

Who doth permit the base contagious clouds

To smother up his beauty from the world,

That, when he please again to be himself,

Being wanted, he may be more wonder'd at,

By breaking through the foul and ugly mists

Of vapours that did seem to strangle him.

So, when this loose behaviour I throw off,

And pay the debts I never promisèd,

By how much better than my word I am,

By so much shall I falsify men's hopes ;

And, like bright metal on a sullen ground,

My reformation, glittering o'er my fault,

Shall show more goodly and attract more eyes

Than that which hath no foil to set it off.

I'll so offend to make offence a skill;
Redeeming time when men think least I will.

[Exit.

SCENE II.—THE ROAD BY GADSHILL.

Enter PRINCE OF WALES, *and* POINS, *disguised.*

Poins. Come, shelter, shelter; I have removed Falstaff's horse, and he frets like a
gummed velvet.

Prince. Stand close.

[Both retire into back scene.

Enter FALSTAFF, *disguised.*

Fal. Poins! Poins, and be hanged! Poins!

Prince [*coming forward*].   Peace, ye fat-
kidneyed rascal: what a brawling dost thou
keep!

Fal. Where's Poins, Hal?

Prince. He is walked up to the top of the
hill: I'll go seek him.

[Retires again into background.

Fal. I am accursed, to rob in that thief's company : the rascal hath removed my horse, and tied him I know not where. If I travel but four foot by the square further a-foot, I shall break my wind. Well, I doubt not but to die a fair death, for all this, if I 'scape hanging for killing that rogue. I have forsworn his company hourly any time this two-and-twenty years, and yet I am bewitched with the rogue's company. If the rascal have not given me medicines to make me love him, I'll be hanged; it could not be else ; I have drunk medicines.— Poins !—Hal !—a plague upon you both ! Bardolph !—Peto !—I'll starve, ere I'll rob a foot further. An 'twere not as good a deed as drink, to turn true man, and leave these rogues, I am the veriest varlet that ever chewed with a tooth. Eight yards of uneven ground, is three score and ten miles a-foot with me : and the stony-hearted villains know it well enough : a plague upon't, when thieves cannot be true to

one another !— [*they whistle*] — Whew !— A
plague upon you all ! Give me my horse, you
rogues ; give me my horse, and be hanged !

Prince [*advances*]. Peace ! lie down ; lay
thine ear close to the ground, and list if thou
canst hear the tread of travellers.

Fal. Have you any levers to lift me up
again, being down? 'Sblood, I'll not bear
mine own flesh so far a-foot again, for all the
coin in thy father's exchequer.—What a plague
mean ye, to colt me thus?

Prince. Thou liest, thou art not colted, thou
art uncolted.

Fal. I pr'ythee, good Prince Hal, help me
to my horse—good king's son.

Prince. Out, you rogue ! shall I be your
ostler ?

Fal. Go, hang thyself in thy own heir-
apparent garters ! If I be ta'en, I'll 'peach for
this. An' I have not ballads made on you all,
and sung to filthy tunes, let a cup of sack be

my poison. When a jest is so forward, and a-foot too !—I hate it.

Enter POINS, GADSHILL, BARDOLPH, *and* PETO, *disguised.*

Gads. Stand.

Fal. So I do, against my will.

Poins. O, 'tis our setter ; I know his voice.

Bard. Case ye, case ye : on with your visards ; there's money of the king's coming down the hill,—'tis going to the king's exchequer.

Fal. You lie, you rogue ; 'tis going to the king's tavern.

Gads. There's enough to make us all !

Fal. To be hanged.

Prince. Sirs, you four shall front them in the narrow lane ; Ned Poins and I will walk lower ; if they 'scape from your encounter, then they light on us.

Fal. But how many be there of them ?

Gads. Some eight or tcn.

Fal. Zounds! will they not rob us?

Prince. What, a coward, Sir John Paunch?

Fal. Indeed, I am not John of Gaunt, your grandfather; but yet no coward, Hal.

Prince. Well, we leave that to the proof.

Poins. Sirrah Jack, thy horse stands behind the hedge; when thou need'st him, there thou shalt find him. Farewell, and stand fast.

Fal. Now cannot I strike him, if I should be hanged.

Prince [*aside*]. Ned, where are our disguises?

Poins [*aside*]. Here, hard by; stand close.

[*Exeunt* PRINCE *and* POINS.

Fal. Now, my masters, happy man be his dole, say I! Every man to his business.

[*They put on their masks, draw their swords, and retire.*

Down with them! cut the villains' throats! Ah! you caterpillars! bacon-fed knaves! they

hate us youth : down with them ! fleece them !
Young men must live. You are grand-jurors,
are ye? We'll jure you, i'faith. [*Exit.*

Enter PRINCE OF WALES *and* POINS, *in buck-
rum suits.*

Prince. The thieves have bound the true
men ; now, could thou and I rob the thieves,
and go merrily to London, it would be argument for a week, laughter for a month, and a
good jest for ever.

Poins. Stand close, I hear them coming.

[*Retire again into the background.*

Enter FALSTAFF, GADSHILL, *and* PETO, *with
bags of money, laughing immoderately.*

Fal. Come, my masters, let us share, and
then to horse before day. An' the Prince and
Poins be not two arrant cowards, there's no
equity stirring : there's no more valour in that
Poins, than in a wild duck.

[PRINCE *and* POINS *advance.*

Prince. Your money !

Poins. Villains.

> [GADSHILL, BARDOLPH, *and* PETO *run
> away, and* FALSTAFF *after a slight
> blow is beaten off by the* PRINCE *and*
> POINS, *he roaring lustily, leaving the
> booty.*

Prince. Got with much ease.   Now merrily
to horse.

The thieves are scatter'd, and possess'd with
fear

So strongly, that they dare not meet each
other ;

Each takes his fellow for an officer.

Away, good Ned.   Falstaff sweats to death,

And lards the lean earth as he walks along :

Were't not for laughing, I should pity him.

Poins. How the rogue roar'd !   [*Exeunt.*

Scene III.—THE BOAR'S HEAD TAVERN, IN
¡EASTCHEAP.

Enter Prince of Wales.

Prince. Ned, pr'ythee come out of that fat
room, and lend me thy hand to laugh a little.

Enter Poins.

Poins. Where hast been, Hal?

Prince. With three or four loggerheads,
amongst three or four score hogsheads. I
have sounded the very base string of humi-
lity. Sirrah, I am sworn brother to a leash
of drawers, and can call them all by their
Christian names, as—Tom, Dick, and Francis.
They take it already upon their salvation, that
though I be but Prince of Wales, yet I am the
king of courtesy; and tell me flatly, I am no
proud Jack, like Falstaff; but a Corinthian, a
lad of mettle, a good boy (so they call me), and
when I am king of England, I shall command
all the good lads in Eastcheap. To conclude, I

am so good a proficient in one quarter of an
hour, that I can drink with any tinker in his
own language during my life.

*   *   *   *   *   *   *

*   *   *Enter* HOSTESS.   *   *

My lord, old Sir John, with half-a-dozen more,
are at the door—shall I let them in ?

*   *   *   *   *   *   *

*   *   *   *   *   *   *

Prince. I pr'ythee call in Falstaff,—call in
ribs—call in tallow.

Enter FALSTAFF, GADSHILL, BARDOLPH, PETO,
     aad DRAWER — *pause* — FALSTAFF *looks*
     angrily at them, then sits.

Poins. Welcome, Jack; whcre hast thou
been ?

Fal. A plague of all cowards, I say, and a vengeance too! marry, and amen. Give me a cup of sack, boy. [*To* DRAWER.] Ere I lead this life long, I'll sew netherstocks, and mend them, and foot them too. A plague of all cowards! Give me a cup of sack, rogue. Is there no virtue extant?

[DRAWER *brings a cup of sack—he drinks.*

Prince [*to* POINS]. Didst thou never see Titan kiss a dish of butter?—pitiful-hearted Titan!—that melted at the sweet tale of the sun? If thou didst, then behold that compound.

Fal. You rogue, here's lime in this sack, too; there is nothing but roguery to be found in villanous man; yet a coward is worse than a cup of sack with lime in it;—a villanous coward! Go thy ways, old Jack; die when thou wilt, if manhood, good manhood, be not forgot upon the face of the earth, then am I a shotten herring. There live not three good men unhanged in England, and one of them is fat, and grows old, heaven help the while! A bad world, I say! A plague of all cowards, I say still!

Prince [*crossing to him*]. How now, woolsack! what mutter you?

Fal. A king's son! If I do not beat thee out of thy kingdom with a dagger of lath, and drive all thy subjects afore thee like a flock of wild geese, I'll never wear hair on my face more. You Prince of Wales!

Prince. Why, you round man—what's the matter?

Fal. Are you not a coward? answer me to that: and Poins there?

Prince. Ye fat paunch, an' ye call me coward, I'll stab thee.

Fal. I call thee coward! I'll see thee hanged, ere I call thee coward; but I would give a thousand pound I could run as fast as thou canst. You are straight enough in the shoulders, you care not who sees your back; call you that backing of your friends? A plague upon such backing! Give me them that will face me; give me [PRINCE *turns to him*]—a cup of sack : I am a rogue if I drunk to-day. [*Exit* BARDOLPH.

Prince. Oh villain! thy lips are scarce wiped since thou drunkest last.

Enter BARDOLPH *with a cup of sack.*

Fal. All's one for that. A plague of all coward's still, say I!
[*Drinks—*BARDOLPH *takes the cup.*

Prince. What's the matter?

Fal. What's the matter? Here be four of us here have ta'en a thousand pound this morning.

Prince. Where is it, Jack? where is it?

Fal. Where is it? taken from us it is; a hundred upon poor four of us.

Prince. What, a hundred, man?

Fal. I am a rogue, if I were not at half-sword with a dozen of them two hours together. I have 'scaped by miracle. I am eight times thrust through the doublet; four through the hose; my buckler cut through and through; my sword hacked like a hand-saw,— *ecce signum.* [*Shows his sword.*] I never dealt better since I was a man: all would not do. A plague of all cowards!—let them speak; if they speak more or less than truth, they are villains, and the sons of darkness.

Prince. Speak, sirs :—[to GADSHILL, &c.,]— how was it?

Bard. We four set upon some dozen—

Fal. Sixteen, at least, my lord.

Bard. And bound them.

Gads. No, no;—they were not bound.

Fal. You rogue, they were bound, every man of them; or I am a Jew else, an Ebrew Jew.

Gads. As we were sharing, some six or seven fresh men set upon us——

Fal. And unbound the rest, and then come in the other.

Prince. What, fought ye with them all?

Fal. All? I know not what ye call all; but I fought not with fifty of them, I am a bunch of radish; if there were not two or three and fifty upon poor old Jack, then am I no two-legged creature.

Poins. 'Pray heaven, you have not killed some of them.

Fal. Nay, that's past praying for; I have peppered two of them: two, I am sure, I have paid; two rogues in buckram suits. I tell thee what, Hal—if I tell thee a lie, spit in my face, call me horse—Thou knowest my old ward—here I lay, and thus I bore my point: four rogues in buckram let drive at me——

Prince. What, four? thou saidst but two, even now.

Fal. Four, Hal—I told thee, four.

Poins. Ay, ay,—he said four.

Fal. These four came all afront, and mainly thrust at me: I made no more ado, but took all their seven points in my target, thus.

Prince. Seven! why, there were but four, even now.

Fal. In buckram.

Poins. Ay, four in buckram suits.

Fal. Seven, by these hilts, or I'm a villain else.

Prince. Pr'ythee, let him alone; we shall have more anon.

Fal. Dost thou hear me, Hal?

Prince. Ay, and mark thee too, Jack.

Fal. Do so; for it is worth the listening to. These nine in buckram, that I told thee of——

Prince. So, two more already.

Fal. Their points being broken——

Poins. Down fell their hose.

Fal. Began to give me ground; but I followed me close, came in foot and hand; and with a thought seven of the eleven I paid.

Prince. Oh, monstrous! eleven buckram men grown out of two!

Fal. But, as the devil would have it, three knaves in Kendal green, came at my back, and let drive at me;—for it was so dark, Hal, that thou couldst not see thy hand.

Prince. These lies are like the father of them; gross as a mountain, open, palpable. Why, thou clay-brained knot-pated fool, thou greasy tallow-ketch——

Fal. What, art thou mad? art thou mad? is not the truth the truth?

Prince. Why, how couldst thou know these men in Kendal green, when it was so dark thou couldst not see thy hand? Come, tell us your reason: what sayest thou to this?

Poins. Come, your reason, Jack, your reason.

Fal. What, upon compulsion? No: were I

at the strappado, or all the racks in the world,
I would not tell you on compulsion. Give you
a reason on compulsion! If reasons were as
plenty as blackberries, I would give no man a
reason upon compulsion, I.

Prince. I'll be no longer guilty of this sin;
this sanguine coward, this horseback-breaker,
this huge hill of flesh—

Fal. Away, you starveling, you eel-skin, you
dried neat's tongue, you stock-fish—Oh, for
breath to utter what is like thee!—you
tailor's yard, you sheath, you bow-case, you
vile standing tuck—   [*Puffing.*

Prince. Well, breathe awhile, and then to it
again; and, when thou hast tired thyself in
base comparisons, hear me speak but this.

Poins. Mark, Jack.

Prince. We two saw you four set on four:
you bound them, and were masters of their
wealth. Mark now, how plain a tale shall put
you down. Then did we two set on you four;

and, with a word, outfaced you from your
prize, and have it; yea, and can show it you
here in the house :—and, Falstaff, you carried
your fat away as nimbly, with as quick dex-
terity, and roared for mercy, and still ran and
roared, as ever I heard bullcalf. What a slave
art thou, to hack thy sword as thou hast done,
and then say, it was in fight! What trick,
what device, what starting-hole, canst thou
now find out, to hide thee from this open and
apparent shame?

Poins. Come, let's hear, Jack,—what trick
hast thou now?

Fal. By the lord, I knew ye! as well as he
that made ye. Why—hear ye, my masters—
was it for me to kill the heir apparent? should
I turn upon the true prince? Why, thou
knowest, I am as valiant as Hercules: but be-
ware instinct: the lion will not touch the true
prince. Instinct is a great matter; I was a
coward on instinct. I shall think the better

of myself and thee duriug my life; I, for a valiant lion, and thou for a true prince. But, lads, I am glad you have the money. Hostess [*calls*], clap-to the doors; watch to-night, pray to-morrow. Gallants, lads, boys, hearts of gold, all the titles of true fellowship come to you. What, shall we be merry? shall we have a play extempore?

Prince. Content: and the argument shall be thy running away.

Fal. Ah, no more of that, Hal, an' thou lovest me.

Enter Hostess.

Hostess. My lord, the prince——

Prince. How now, my lady, the hostess? what sayest thou to me?

Hostess. Marry, my lord, there is a nobleman of the court at door, would speak with you; he says, he comes from your father.

Prince. Give him as much as will make him

a royal man, and send him back again to my mother.

Fal. What manner of man is he?

Hostess. An old man.

Fal. What doth gravity out of bed at mid-night?—Shall I give him his answer?

Prince. Pr'ythee do, Jack.

Fal. 'Faith, and I'll send him packing.

[*Exeunt* FALSTAFF *and* Hostess.

Prince. Now, sirs: [*to* BARDOLPH, &c.] by'r lady, you fought fair; so did you, Peto; so did you, Bardolph; you are lions too, you ran away upon instinct; you will not touch the true prince; no—fie!

Bard. 'Faith, I ran, when I saw others run.

Prince. Tell me now, in earnest—how came Falstaff's sword so hacked?

Bard. Why, he hacked it with his dagger; and said, he would swear truth out of England, but he would make you believe it was done in fight; and persuaded us to do the like. Yea, and to tickle our noses with spear grass, to make them bleed; and then to beslubber our garmeuts with it, and to swear, it was the blood of true men; I did that, I did not these seven years before, I—blushed to hear his monstrous devices.

Prince. O, villain! thou stolest a cup of sack eighteen years ago, and wert taken with the manner, and ever since thou hast blushed extempore: thou hadst fire and sword on thy side, and yet thou ran'st away:—what instinct hadst thou for it?

Bard. My lord, do you see these meteors? do you behold these exhalations?

[*Pointing to his own face.*

Prince. I do.

Bard. What think you they portend?

Prince. Hot livers, and cold purses.

Bard. Choler, my lord, if rightly taken.

Prince. No, if rightly taken—halter. Here comes lean Jack, here comes bare-bone.

Enter FALSTAFF.

How now, my sweet creature of bombast?
How long is't ago, Jack, since thou saw'st
thine own knee?

Fal Mine own knee? When I was about
thy years, Hal, I was not an eagle's talon in
the waist; I could have crept into an alder-
man's thumb-ring: a plague of sighing and
grief! it blows a man up like a bladder. * *
There's villanous news abroad: here was Sir
John Bracy from your father; you must to
the court in the morning. Thou wilt be hor- *
ribly chid to-morrow, when thou com'st to thy
father : if thou love me, practise an answer.

Prince. Do thou stand for my father, and
examine me upon the particulars of my
life.

Fal. Shall I? content :—this chair shall be

* This portion of the scene is sometimes omitted in representation.

my state, this dagger my sceptre, and this cushion my crown.

Prince. Thy state is taken for a joint-stool, thy golden sceptre for a leaden dagger, and thy precious rich crown, for a pitiful bald crown!

Fal. Well, an' the fire of grace be not quite out of thee, now shalt thou be moved. Give me a cup of sack, to make mine eyes look red, that it may be thought I have wept; for I must speak in passion, and I will do it in King Cambyses' vein.

Enter Hostess *with sack.*

Prince. Well, here is my leg.

Fal. And here is my speech:—Stand aside, nobility.

Hostess. This is excellent sport, i'faith.

Fal. Weep not, sweet queen, for trickling tears are vain.

Hostess. O the father! how he holds his countenance.

Fal. For heaven's sake, lords, convey my tristful queen, for tears do stop the flood-gates of her eyes.

Hostess. O rare! he doth it as like one of these harlotry players, as ever I see.

Fal. Peace, good pint-pot; peace, good tickle-brain.—Harry, I do not only marvel where thou spendest thy time, but also how thou art accompanied; for though the camomile, the more it is trodden on, the faster it grows, yet youth, the more it is wasted, the sooner it wears. That thou art my son, I have partly thy mother's word, partly my own opinion that doth warrant me. If then thou be son to me, here lies the point;—Why, being son to me, art thou so pointed at? Shall the blessed sun of heaven prove a micher, and eat blackberries? a question not to be ask'd. Shall the son of England prove a thief, and take purses? a question to be ask'd. There is a thing, Harry, which thou hast often heard of, and it is known to many in our land by the name of pitch: this pitch, as ancient writers do report, doth ·defile; so doth the company thou keepest. * * * * And yet there is a virtuous man, whom I have often noted in thy company, but I know not his name.

Prince. What manner of man, an' it like your majesty?

Fal. A good portly man, i'faith, and a corpulent; of a cheerful look, a pleasing eye, and a most noble carriage; and, as I think, his age some fifty, or, by'r lady, inclining to three-score; and now I remember me, his name is Falstaff; if that man should be lewdly given, he deceiveth me; for, Harry, I see virtue in his looks. Him keep with, the rest banish. And tell me now, thou naughty varlet, tell me, where hast thou been this month?

Prince. Dost thou speak like a king? Do thou stand for me, and I'll play my father.·

Fal. Depose me? If thou dost it half so gravely, so majestically, both in word and matter, hang me up by the heels for a rabbit-sucker, or a poulterer's hare. ·

Prince. Well, here I am set.   [*Sits.*

Fal. And here I stand :—judge, my masters.

Prince. Now Harry? whence come you?

Fal. My noble lord, from Eastcheap.

Prince. The complaints I hear of thee are grievous.

Fal. 'Sblood, my lord, they are false :—nay, I'll tickle ye for a young prince, i'faith.

Prince. Swearest thou, ungracious boy? henceforth ne'er look on me. Thou art violently carried away from grace : there is a devil haunts thee, in the likeness of a fat old man : a tun of man is thy companion.   *   *   *·
Wherein is he good, but to taste sack and drink it? wherein neat and cleanly, but to carve a capon and eat it? wherein cunning, but in craft? wherein crafty, but in villany?

wherein villanous, but in all things? wherein worthy, but in nothing?

Fal. I would your grace would take me with you;—Whom means your grace?

Prince. That villanous abominable misleader of youth, Falstaff, that old white-bearded Satan.

Fal. My lord, the man I know.

Prince. I know thou dost.

Fal. But to say, I know more harm in him than in myself, were to say more than I know. That he is old, (the more the pity,) his white hairs do witness it: but that he is (saving your reverence,) a villain, that I utterly deny. If sack and sugar be a fault, heaven help the wicked! If to be fat be to be hated, then Pharaoh's lean kine are to be loved. No, my good lord; banish Peto, banish Bardolph, banish Poins; but for sweet Jack Falstaff, kind Jack Falstaff, true Jack Falstaff, valiant Jack Falstaff, and therefore more valiant, being, as he is, old Jack Falstaff, banish not him thy

Harry's company, banish not him thy Harry's company; banish plump Jack, and banish all the world.

Prince.—I do, I will.   [*A knocking heard.*

The Hostess *goes off, and immediately re-enters.*

Hostess. O, my lord, my lord!

Fal. Heigh, heigh! the devil rides upon a fiddle-stick.   What's the matter?

Hostess. The sheriff and all the watch are at the door: they are come to search the house. Shall I let them in?

[PRINCE *motions* "yes."]   [*Exit* Hostess.

Fal. Hal, thou art essentially mad, without seeming so.

Prince. And thou a natural coward, without instinct.

Fal. I deny your major: if you will deny the sheriff, so; if not, let him enter: if I become not a cart as well as another man, a plague on my bringing up! I hope, I shall as soon be strangled with a halter, as another.

Prince. Go, hide thee behind the arras; the rest walk up above.—Now, my masters, for a true face and a good conscience.

Fal. Both which I have had; but their date is out, and therefore I'll hide me.　　[*Retires.*

Prince. [POINS *takes paper from* FALSTAFF'S *pocket.*] What hast thou found?

Poins. Nothing but papers, my lord.

Prince. Let's see what they be.　　[*Reads.*

Item, a capon,	2*s.* 2*d.*
Item, sauce,	4*d.*
Item, sack, two gallons,	5*s.* 8*d.*
Item, anchovies and sack, after supper,	2*s.* 6*d.*
Item, bread, a halfpenny.	

O, monstrous! but one half-penny worth of bread to this intolerable deal of sack!—What there is else, keep close; we'll read it at more advantage; there let him sleep till day. I'll to the court in the morning: we must all to the wars, and thy place shall be honourable. I'll procure this fat rogue a charge of foot; and, I

know, his death will be a march of twelvescore.
The money shall be paid back again, with
advantage. Be with me betimes in the morning; and so, good morrow, Poins. [*Exit.*

Poins. Good morrow, good my lord. [*Exit.*

SCENE IV.—THE BOAR'S HEAD TAVERN, IN
EASTCHEAP.

Enter FALSTAFF *and* BARDOLPH *with two
tankards.*

Fal. Bardolph, am I not fallen away vilely,
since this last action? do I not bate? do I not
dwindle?—why, my skin hangs about me like
an old lady's loose gown; I am withered like
an old apple-john. [*sits.*] Well, I'll repent, and
that suddenly, while I am in some liking; I
shall be out of heart shortly, and then I shall
have no strength to repent. An' I have not

forgotten what the inside of a church is made of, I am a peppercorn, a brewer's horse. Company, villanous company, hath been the spoil of me.

Bard. Sir John, you are so fretful, you cannot live long.

Fal. Why, there is it;—come, sing me a vile song; make me merry. I was as virtuously given as a gentleman need to be; virtuous enough; swore little; diced, not above seven times a week; paid money that I borrowed—three or four times; lived well, and in good compass; and now I live out of all order, out of all compass.

Bard. Why, you are so fat, Sir John, that you must needs be out of all compass—out of all reasonable compass, Sir John.

[Falstaff *rises*.

Fal. Do thou amend thy face, and I'll amend my life: thou art our admiral—thou bearest

the lantern in the poop,* but 'tis in the nose
of thee; thou art the Knight of the Burning
Lamp.

Bard. Why, Sir John, my face does you no
harm.

Fal. No, I'll be sworn; I make as good use
of it as many a man doth of a death's head,
or a *memento mori.*   *   *   *   Thou art altogether given over; and wert indeed, but for
the light in thy face, the son of utter darkness.
When thou rannest up Gadshill in the night to
catch my horse, if I did not think thou hadst
been an *ignis fatuus,* or a ball of wildfire,
there's no purchase in money. O, thou art a
perpetual triumph, an everlasting bonfire-light!
Thou hast saved me a thousand marks in links
and torches, walking with thee in the night betwixt tavern and tavern : but the sack that thou
hast drunk me would have bought me lights as
good cheap at the dearest chandler's in Europe.

* Collier's "Emendations"—*not in the poop.*

16

I have maintained that salamander of yours with fire any time this two-and-thirty years; heaven reward me for it!

Bard. 'Sblood, I would my face were in your body!

Fal. Lud-a-mercy! so should I be sure to be heart-burned.

Enter Hostess.

How now, dame Partlet the hen! have you en-quired yet who picked my pocket?

Hostess. Why, Sir John! what do you think, Sir John? do you think I keep thieves in my house? I have searched, I have en-quired, so has my husband, man by man, boy by boy, servant by servant; the tithe of a hair was never lost in my house before.

Fal. Ye lie, hostess; Bardolph was shaved, and lost many a hair; and I'll be sworn my pocket was picked: Go to, you are a woman, go.

Hostess. Who, I? no;—I defy thee : Odd's light, I was never called so in mine own house before.

Fal. Go to; I know you well enough.

Hostess. No, Sir John; you do not know me, Sir John; I know you, Sir John; you owe me money, Sir John, and now you pick a quarrel to beguile me of it: I bought you a dozen of shirts to your back.

Fal. Dowlas, filthy dowlas; I have given them away to bakers' wives, and they have made bolters of them.

Hostess. Now, as I am a true woman, holland of eight shillings an ell. You owe money here, besides, Sir John, for your diet and by-drinkings; and money lent you, four-and-twenty pounds.

Fal. [*pointing to* BARDOLPH.] He had his part of it; let him pay.

Hostess. He! alas, he is poor: he hath nothing.

Fal. How! poor? Look upon his face; what call you rich? Let them coin his nose; let them coin his cheeks; I'll not pay a denier. What, will you make a younker of me? Shall I not take mine ease in mine inn, but I shall have my pocket picked? I have lost a seal-ring of my grandfather's, worth forty mark.

Hostess. O! I have heard the prince tell him, I know not how oft, that that ring was copper.

Fal. How! the prince is a jack, a sneak-cup; and if he were here, I would cudgel him like a dog, if he would say so.

Enter PRINCE OF WALES *in half armour, marching.*

How now, lad? is the wind in that door, i'faith?—must we all march?

Bard. Yea, two and two, Newgate-fashion.

Hostess. My lord, I pray you, hear me.

Prince. What say'st thou, mistress Quickly?

How does thy husband? I love him well, he is an honest man.

Hostess. Good my lord, hear me.

Fal. Pr'ythee, let her alone, and list to me.

Prince. What say'st thou, Jack?

Fal. The other night, I fell asleep here behind the arras, and had my pocket picked.

Prince. What didst thou lose, Jack?

Fal. Wilt thou believe, me Hal? Three or four bonds of forty pounds a-piece, and a seal-ring of my grandfather's.

Prince. A trifle, some eight-penny matter.

Hostess. So I told him, my lord; and I said, I heard your grace say so: and, my lord, he speaks most vilely of you, like a foul-mouthed man as he is; and said he would cudgel you.

Prince. What! he did not?

Hostess. There's neither faith, truth, nor womanhood in me else.

Fal. There's no more faith in thee than in a stewed prune: nor no more truth in thee than

in a drawn fox; and for womanhood, Maid
Marian may be the deputy's wife of the ward
to thee. Go, thou thing, go.

Hostess. Say, what thing? what thing?

Fal. What thing? Why, a thing to thank
heav'n on.

Hostess. I am no thing to thank heaven on,
I would thou shouldst know it; I am an honest
man's wife; and, setting thy knighthood aside,
thou art a knave to call me so.

Prince. Thou say'st true, hostess, and he
slanders thee most grossly.

Hostess. So he doth you, my lord! and said,
this other day, you owed him a thousand
pound.

Prince. Sirrah! do I owe a thousand pound?

Fal. A thousand pound, Hal? a million;
thy love is worth a million; thou owest me
thy love.

Hostess. Nay, my lord, he called you Jack,
and said, he would cudgel you.

Fal. Did I, Bardolph?

Bard. Indeed, Sir John, you said so.

Fal. Yea! if he said my ring was copper.

Prince. I say it is copper; darest thou be as good as thy word now?

Fal. Why, Hal, thou knowest, as thou art but man, I dare; but, as thou art Prince, I fear thee, as I fear the roaring of the lion's whelp.

Prince. And why not, as the lion?

Fal. The king himself is to be feared as the lion: dost thou think I'll fear thee as I fear thy father? nay, an' I do, let my girdle break!

Prince. Charge an honest woman with picking thy pocket! Why, thou impudent, embossed rascal, if there were anything in thy pocket, but tavern-reckonings, and one poor pennyworth of sugar-candy, to make thee long-winded; if thy pocket were enriched with any other injuries but these, I am a villain:

and yet you will stand to it, you will not pocket-up wrong: art thou not ashamed?

Fal. Dost thou hear, Hal? Thou knowest, in the state of innocency, Adam fell; and what should poor Jack Falstaff do, in the days of villany? Thou seest, I have more flesh than another man: and therefore more frailty. You confess, then, you picked my pocket?

Prince. It appears so by the story.

Fal. Hostess, I forgive thee: go, make ready breakfast: love thy husband, look to thy servants, cherish thy guests: thou shalt find me tractable to any honest reason: thou seest, I am pacified. Still?—Nay, pr'ythee, be gone. [*Kisses her.*] [*Exit* Hostess.

Now, Hal, to the news at court:—for the robbery, lad—how is that answered?

Prince. The money is paid back again.

Fal. O, I do not like that paying back; 'tis a double labour.

Prince. I am good friends with my father, and may do anything.

Fal. Rob me the exchequer the first thing thou dost, and do it with unwashed hands too.

Bard. [*eagerly*]. Do, my lord.

Prince. I have procured thee, Jack, a charge of foot.

Fal. I would it had been of horse. Where shall I find one that can steal well? Oh, for a fine thief, of the age of two-and-twenty, or thereabouts! I am heinously unprovided. Well, heaven be thanked for these rebels, they offend none but the virtuous: I laud them, I praise them.

Prince. Bardolph—

Bard. My lord.

Prince. Go, bear this letter to lord John of Lancaster, My brother John; this to my lord of Westmoreland. [*Exit* BARDOLPH.

Jack,—meet me to-morrow in the Temple-hall, At two o'clock i' the afternoon:

There shalt thou know thy charge; and there
   receive
Money, and order for their furniture.   [*Going.*
The land is burning; Percy stands on high:
And either they or we must lower lie.   [*Exit.*
   Fal. Rare words! brave world!—Hostess,
     my breakfast, come :—
O, I could wish this tavern were my drum!

AN INTERVAL OF TEN MINUTES.

SELECTED SCENES

FROM

KING HENRY THE FOURTH.

PART II.

SCENE I.—THE ROAD NEAR COVENTRY.

Enter FALSTAFF *and* BARDOLPH, *in half armour.*

Fal. Bardolph, get thee before to Coventry;
fill me a bottle of sack; our soldiers shall march
through; we'll to Sutton-Colfield to-night.

Bard. Will you give me money, captain?

Fal. Lay out, lay out.

Bard. This bottle makes an angel.

Fal. An' it do take it for thy labour; and, if
it make twenty, take them all; I'll answer the
coinage. Bid my lieutenant Peto meet me at
the town's end.

Bard. I will, captain: farewell. [*Exit.*

Fal. If I be not ashamed of my soldiers, I am a souced gurnet. I have misused the king's press vilely. I have got, in exchange of a hundred and fifty soldiers, three hundred and odd pounds. I press me none but good householders, yeomen's sons: inquire me out contracted bachelors, such as had been asked twice on the banns; such a commodity of warm slaves, as had as lief hear the devil as a drum; such as fear the report of a caliver, worse than a struck fowl, or a hurt wild duck. I press me none but such toasts-and-butter, with hearts no bigger than pins' heads, and they have bought out their services; and now my whole charge consists of ancients, corporals, lieutenants, gentlemen of companies, slaves as ragged as Lazarus in the painted cloth; and such as, indeed, were never soldiers; but discarded unjust serving-men, younger sons to younger brothers, revolted tapsters, and ostlers trade-fallen, the cankers of a calm world and a

long peace: and such have I, to fill up the
rooms of them that have bought out their services, that you would think, I had a hundred
and fifty tattered prodigals lately come from
swine-keeping, from eating draff and husks. A
mad fellow met me on the way, and told me, I
had unloaded all the gibbets, and pressed the
dead bodies. No eye hath seen such scare-
crows! I'll not march through Coventry with
them, that's flat. Nay, and the villains march
wide betwixt the legs, as if they had gyves on;
for, indeed, I had the most of them out of
prison. There's but a shirt and a half in all
my company; and the half shirt is two napkins
tacked together, and thrown over the shoulders
like a herald's coat without sleeves; and the
shirt, to say the truth, stolen from my host of
St. Alban's, or the red-nose innkeeper of Dain-
try. But that's all one; they'll find linen
enough on every hedge.

Enter PRINCE OF WALES.

Prince. How now, blown Jack? how now, quilt?

Fal. What, Hal? How now, mad wag? what dost thou in Warwickshire? * * * I thought thou hadst already been at Shrewsbury.

* *Prince.* 'Faith, 'tis more than time that I were there, and you too: but my powers are there already. The king, I can tell you, looks for us all; we must away all night.

Fal. Tut, never fear me; I am as vigilant as a cat to steal cream.

Prince. I think, to steal cream, indeed; for thy theft hath already made thee butter. But tell me, Jack—whose fellows are those that come after?

Fal. Mine, Hal, mine.

Prince. I did never see such pitiful rascals.

Fal. Tut, tut; good enough to toss; food

---

* This speech, and one other marked *, should be spoken by the Earl of Westmoreland.

for powder, food for powder; they'll fill a pit as well as better; tush, man,—mortal men, mortal men.

* Prince. Ay, but methinks they are exceedingly poor and bare,—too beggarly.

Fal. 'Faith, for their poverty—I know not where they had that; and for their bareness— I· am sure, they never learnt that of me.

Prince. No, I'll be sworn; unless you call three fingers on the ribs, bare. But, sirrah, make haste; Percy is already in the field.

Fal. What, is the king encamped?

Prince. He is; I fear we shall stay too long.

Fal. Well,

To the latter end of a fray, and the beginning
  of a feast,

Fits a dull fighter, and a keen guest.

    *   *   *   *   *   *   *

Fal. Hal, if thou see me down in the battle, and bestride me, so : 'tis a point of friendship.

Prince. Nothing but a Colossus can do thee that friendship. Say thy prayers, and farewell.

Fal. I would it were bed-time, Hal, and all well.

Prince. Why, thou owest heav'n a death.

[*Exit.*

Fal. 'Tis not due yet; I would be loth to pay him before his day. What need I be so forward with him that calls not on me? Well, 'tis no matter: Honour pricks me on. Yea, but how if honour prick me off when I come on? How then? Can honour set to a leg? No. Or an arm? No. Or take away the grief of a wound? No. Honour hath no skill in surgery then? No. What is honour? A word. What is that word honour? Air. A trim reckoning! Who hath it? He that died o' Wednesday. Doth he feel it? No. Doth he hear it? No. Is it insensible, then? Yea, to the dead. But will it not live with the living? No. Why? Detraction will not suffer

it:—therefore I'll none of it. Honour is a mere scutcheon; and so ends my catechism.
[*Exit.*

SCENE II.—A STREET IN LONDON.

Enter SIR JOHN FALSTAFF, *and* ROBIN, *his page, following him with his sword and buckler.*

Fal. Sirrah, you giant, what says the doctor?
Page. He said, sir, you might have more diseases than he knew for.
Fal. Men of all sorts take a pride to gird at me. The brain of this foolish-compounded clay, man, is not able to invent anything that tends to laughter, more than I invent, or is invented on me: I am not only witty in myself, but the cause that wit is in other men. I do here walk before thee, like a sow, that hath overwhelmed all her litter but one. If the

17

prince put thee into my service for any other reason than to set me off, why then I have no judgment. Thou mandrake, thou art fitter to be worn in my cap, than to wait at my heels. I was never manned with an agate till now; but I will set you neither in gold nor silver, but in vile apparel, and send you back again to your master for a jewel—the juvenal, the prince, your master, whose chin is not yet fledged. I will sooner have a beard grow in the palm of my hand than he shall get one on his cheek; and yet he will be crowing as if he had writ man ever since his father was a bachelor. He may keep his own grace, but he is almost out of mine, I can assure him. What said Master Dumbleton about the satin for my short cloak and my slops?

Page. He said, sir, you should procure him better assurance than Bardolph; he would not take his bond and yours; he lik'd not the security.

Fal. A rascally yea-forsooth knave! to bear a gentleman in hand, and then stand upon security!—I had as lief they would put rats-bane in my mouth, as offer to stop it with security. I look'd he should have sent me two-and-twenty yards of satin, as I am a true knight, and he sends me security. Well, he may sleep in security. * * * * Where's Bardolph?

Page. He's gone to Smithfield, to buy your worship a horse.

Fal. I bought him in Paul's, and he'll buy me a horse in Smithfield: an' I could get me but a wife in the stews, I were manned, horsed, and wived.

Page. Sir, here comes the nobleman that committed the prince for striking him about Bardolph.

Fal. Wait close, I will not see him.

Enter the Lord Chief Justice, Gower *and two* Apparitors.

Chief J. What's he that goes there?

Gower. Falstaff, an't please your worship.

Chief J. He that was in question for the robbery?—Call him back again.

Gower. Sir John Falstaff!

[*Crosses behind to the* Page.

Fal. [*aside to the* Page] Boy, tell him I am deaf.

Page. [*to the* Apparitor.] You must speak louder, my master is deaf.

Chief J. I am sure he is, to the hearing of anything good. Go, pluck him by the elbow,—I must speak with him.

Gower. [*to* Falstaff.] Sir John.

Fal. What, a young knave, and beg! Is there not war? Is there not employment? Doth not the king lack subjects? Do not the rebels need soldiers? Though it be a shame to be on any side but one, it is worse shame to beg than to be on the worst side, were it worse than the name of rebellion can tell how to make it.

Gower. You mistake me, sir.

Fal. Why, sir, did I say you were an honest man? Setting my knighthood and my soldiership aside, I had lied in my throat, if I had said so.

Gower. I pray you, sir, then set your knighthood and your soldiership aside; and give me leave to tell you, you lie in your throat, if you say I am any other than an honest man.

Fal. I give thee leave to tell me so! I lay aside that which grows to me! If thou get'st any leave of me, hang me; if thou takest leave, thou wert better be hanged. You hunt-counter, hence! avaunt!

Gower. Sir, my lord would speak with you.

Chief J. [*crosses.*] Sir John Falstaff, a word with you.

Fal. My good lord! Give your lordship good time of day. I am glad to see your lordship abroad: I heard say your lordship was sick; I hope your lordship goes abroad by advice. Your lordship, though not clean past your youth, hath yet some smack of age in you, some relish of the saltness of time; and I most humbly beseech your lordship to have a reverend care of your health.

Chief J. Sir John, I sent for you before your expedition to Shrewsbury.

Fal. An't please your lordship, I hear His Majesty is return'd with some discomfit from Wales.

Chief J. I talk not of His Majesty—you would not come when I sent for you.

Fal. And I hear, moreover, his highness is fallen into this same apoplexy.

Chief J. Well, heaven mend him!—I pray, let me speak with you.

Fal. This apoplexy is, as I take it, a kind of lethargy, an't please your lordship, a kind of sleeping in the blood, a tingling——

Chief J. What tell you me of it? be it as it is.

Fal. It hath its original from much grief; from study, and perturbation of the brain: I have read the cause of his effects in Galen; it is a kind of deafness.

Chief J. I think you are fallen into the disease, for you hear not what I say to you.

Fal. Very well, my lord, very well: rather, an't please you, it is the disease of not listening, the malady of not marking, that I am troubled withal.

Chief J. To punish you by the heels, would amend the attention of your ears: and I care not, if I do become your physician.

Fal. I am as poor as Job, my lord: but not

so patient: your lordship may administer the potion of imprisonment to me, in respect of poverty; but how I should be your patient to follow your prescriptions, the wise may make some drachm of a scruple, or, indeed, a scruple itself.

Chief J. I sent for you when there were matters against you for your life, to come to speak with me.

Fal. As I was then advised, by my learned counsel in the laws of this land-service, I did not come.

Chief J. Well, the truth is, Sir John, you live in great infamy.

Fal. He that buckles him in my belt, cannot live in less.

Chief. J. Your means are very slender, and your waste is great.

Fal. I would it were otherwise; I would my means were greater, and my waist slenderer.

Chief J. You have misled the youthful prince.

Fal. The young prince hath misled me: I am the fellow with the great body, and he my dog.

Chief J. Well, I am loth to gall a new-healed wound; your day's service at Shrewsbury hath a little gilded over your night's exploit on Gadshill: you may thank the unquiet time for your quiet o'er-posting that action.

Fal. My lord!

Chief J. But since all is well, keep it so: wake not a sleeping wolf.

Fal. To wake a wolf is as bad as to smell a fox.

Chief J. What! you are as a candle, the better part burnt out.

Fal. A wassel candle, my lord; all tallow; if I did say of wax, my growth would approve the truth.

Chief J. There is not a white hair on your face, but should have his effect of gravity.

Fal. His effect of gravy, gravy, gravy.

Chief J. You follow the young prince up and down, like his ill angel.

Fal. Not so, my lord; your ill angel is light; but, I hope, he that looks upon me, will take me without weighing. Virtue is of so little regard in these costermonger times, that true valour is turned bear-herd.   *   *   * You that are old consider not the capacities of us that are young; you do measure the heat of our livers with the bitterness of your galls; and we, that are in the vaward of our youth, I must confess, are wags, too.

Chief J. Do you set down your name in the scroll of youth, that are written down old with all the characters of age? Have you not a moist eye?—A dry hand?—A yellow cheek?— A white beard?—A decreasing leg?—An increasing body? Is not your voice broken?—

Your wind short?—Your chin double?—Your wit single? And every part about you blasted with antiquity? And will you yet call yourself young? Fie, fie, fie, Sir John!

Fal. My lord, I was born about three of the clock in the afternoon, with a white head, and something o' a round body. For my voice—I have lost it with halloaing and singing of anthems. To approve my youth further, I will not: the truth is, I am only old in judgment and understanding; and he that will caper with me for a thousand marks, let him lend me the money, and have at him.—For the box o' the ear that the prince gave you—he gave it like a rude prince, and you took it like a sensible lord. I have check'd him for it, and the young lion repents; marry, not in ashes and sack-cloth, but in new silk and old sack.

Chief J. Well, heaven send the prince a better companion!

Fal. Heaven send the companion a better prince! I cannot rid my hands of him.

Chief J. Well, the king hath sever'd you and Prince Harry; I hear you are going with Lord John of Lancaster, against the Archbishop and the Earl of Northumberland.

Fal. Yea, I thank your pretty sweet wit for it.—There is not a dangerous action can peep out its head, but I am thrust upon it. Well, I cannot last ever: but it was always yet the trick of our English nation, if they have a good thing, to make it too common. If you will needs say, I am an old man, you should give me rest. I would to heaven my name were not so terrible to the enemy as it is! I were better to be eaten to death with rust, than to be scoured to nothing with perpetual motion.

Chief J. Well, be honest, be honest! and heaven bless your expedition!

Fal. Will your lordship lend me a thousand pound, to furnish me forth?

Chief J. Not a penny, not a penny; you are too impatient to bear crosses. Fare you well. —Commend me to my cousin Westmoreland.

[*Exeunt the* CHIEF JUSTICE, GOWER *and* Apparitors.

Fal. If I do, fillip me with a three-man beetle. Boy!

Page. Sir.

Fal. What money is in my purse?

Page. Seven groats and two-pence.

Fal. I can get no remedy against this consumption of the purse: borrowing only lingers and lingers it out, but the disease is incurable. A plague of this gout! it plays the rogue with my great toe. It is no matter if I do halt; I have the wars for my colour, and my pension shall seem the more reasonable. A good wit will make use of anything; I will turn diseases to commodity.

[*Exeunt.*

Enter Hostess, Fang, *and* Snare.

Hostess. Master Fang, have you entered the action against Sir John?

Fang. It is entered　*　*　*

Hostess. I am undone by his going; I warrant you, he's an infinitive thing upon my score:—good master Fang, hold him sure— good master Snare, let him not 'scape. He comes continually to Pye Corner (saving your manhoods), to buy a saddle; and he's indited to dinner to the Lubber's Head, in Lumbart Street, to Master Smooth's, the silkman. A hundred mark is a long loan for a poor lone woman to bear; and I have borne, and borne, and borne; and have been fubbed off, and fubbed off, and fubbed off, from this day to that day, that it is a shame to be thought on. Yonder he comes; and that arrant malmsey-nose knave, Bardolph, with him. Do your offices, do your offices, Master Fang and Master Snare; do me, do me, do me your offices.

Enter SIR JOHN FALSTAFF, BARDOLPH, *and the* Page.

Fal. How now! whose mare's dead?— What's the matter?

Fang. (*taps him on shoulder.*) Sir John, I arrest you at the suit of Mrs. Quickly.

Fal. Away, varlets!—Draw, Bardolph! (*puts* BARDOLPH *between himself and* FANG—*scuffle between* BARDOLPH, FANG, SNARE, *and* PAGE.) Cut me off the villain's head—throw her in the channel.

Hostess. Throw me in the channel!— Murder! murder! O, thou honey-suckle villain! wilt thou kill heav'n's officers, and the king's? Oh, thou honey-seed rogue! thou art a honey-seed; a man-queller, and a woman-queller.

Fal. Keep them off, Bardolph.

Fang. A rescue! a rescue!

Hostess. Good people, bring a rescue or two.
Thou wo't, wo't thou!—Thou wo't, wo't thou?
—Do, do, thou rogue! do, thou hemp-seed!

Fal. Away, you scullion! you rampallian!
you fustilarian! I'll tickle your catastrophe.

Enter the LORD CHIEF JUSTICE *and two*
Apparitors.

Chief J. What's the matter?—Keep the
peace here, ho! (BARDOLPH *and* PAGE, *seeing
the* CHIEF JUSTICE, *run behind,*—FANG *and*
SNARE *seize hold of* FALSTAFF.)

Hostess. Good, my lord, be good to me, I
beseech you.

Chief J. How now, Sir John?—What, are
you brawling here? Doth this become your
place, your time, and business? You should
have been well on your way to York. Stand

from him, fellow! wherefore hangs't thou on him?

Hostess. O, my most worshipful lord, an't please your grace, I am a poor widow of East-cheap, and he is arrested at my suit. (FANG *and* SNARE *go behind, next to the* Page *and* BARDOLPH.)

Chief J. For what sum?

Hostess. It is more than for some, my lord; it is for all, all I have: he hath eaten me out of house and home.

Chief J. How comes this, Sir John? Fie! What man of good temper would endure this tempest of exclamation? Are you not ashamed to enforce a poor widow to so rough a course to come by her own?

Fal. What is the gross sum that I owe thee? (*crossing.*)

Hostess. Marry, if thou wert an honest man, thyself, and the money, too. Thou didst swear to me upon a parcel-gilt goblet, sitting in my

Dolphin Chamber, at the round table, by a sea-coal fire, on Wednesday, in Whitsun-week, when the prince broke thy head for liking his father to a singing-man at Windsor—thou didst swear to me then, as I was washing thy wound, to marry me, and make me, my lady, thy wife. * * * And didst thou not kiss me, and bid me fetch thee thirty shillings? —I put thee now to thy book-oath, deny it if thou canst.

Fal. My lord, this is a poor mad soul; and she says, up and down the town, that her eldest son is like you; she hath been in good case, and, the truth, is, poverty hath distracted her. But for these foolish officers, I beseech you, I may have redress against them.

Chief J. Sir John, Sir John, I am well acquainted with your manner of wrenching the true cause the false way. It is not a confident brow, nor the throng of words that come with such more than impudent sauciness from you, can thrust me from a level consideration : you have, as it appears to me, practised upon the easy-yielding spirit of this woman. * * *

Fal. My lord, I will not undergo this sneap without reply. You call honourable boldness impudent sauciness : if a man will make court'sy, and say nothing, he is virtuous : no, my lord, my humble duty remembered, I will not be your suitor; I say to you, I do desire deliverance from these officers, being upon hasty employment in the king's affairs.

Chief J. You speak as having power to do wrong : but answer in the effect of your reputation, and satisfy the poor woman.

Fal. Come hither, hostess. [*taking her aside.*]

Enter GOWER *with letters.*

Gower. The king, my lord, and Harry Prince of Wales are near at hand; the rest the paper tells.

Fal.)*aside to* HOSTESS.)   As I am a gentleman——

Hostess. Nay, you have said that before.

Fal. As I am a gentleman—come, no more
words of it.

Hostess. By this heavenly ground I tread
on, I must be fain to pawn both my plate and
the tapestry of my dining chambers.

Fal. Glasses, glasses, is the only drinking :
and for the walls—a pretty slight drollery, or
the story of the prodigal in water-work, is
worth a thousand of these fly-bitten tapestries.
Let it be ten pound, if thou canst.   Come, if it
were not for thy humours, there is not a better
wench in England.   Go, wash thy face, and
'draw thy action : come, thou must not be in
this humour with me ; dost not know me?
Come, come, I know thou wast set on to this.
(*holding both her hands and see-sawing her
arms playfully.*)

Hostess. 'Pray thee, Sir John, let it be but

twenty nobles : I am loth to pawn my plate, in good earnest, la.

Fal. Let it alone, I'll make other shift : you'll be a fool still. (*sulkily.*)

Hostess. Well, you shall have it, though I pawn my gown. I hope you'll come to supper. You'll pay me all together.

Fal. Will I live? (*to* BARDOLPH.) Go with her, with her; (*aside*) hook on, hook on.

Exeunt HOSTESS, BARDOLPH, FANG, *and* Page

to house.

Chief J. I have heard better news.

Fal. (*going to him*) What's the news, my lord?

Chief J. (*neglecting him.*) Where lay the king to-night?

Gower. At Basingstoke, my lord.

Fal. I hope, my lord, all's well. Comes the king back from Wales, my noble lord?

Chief J. You shall have letters of me presently.—Come along with me, good Master Gower. (*crosses.*)

Fal. My lord——

Chief J. (*turns.*) What's the matter?

Fal. Master Gower, shall I entreat you with me to dinner?

Gower. I must wait upon my good lord here : I thank you, good Sir John.

Chief J. Sir John, you loiter here too long, being you are to take soldiers up in counties as you go.

Fal. (*pretending not to hear him.*) Will you sup with me, Master Gower?

Chief J. What foolish master taught you these manners, Sir John?

Fal. Master Gower, if they become me not, he was a fool that taught them me. (*crossing, laughing at the* Chief Justice.) This is the right fencing grace, my lord; tap for tap, and so part fair.

Chief J. Now, the Lord lighten thee; thou art a great fool.

Fal. Tap for tap.

Exeunt the CHIEF JUSTICE, *and* Apparitors, FALSTAFF *laughing.*

SCENE IV.—A PUBLIC PLACE NEAR WEST-
MINSTER ABBEY.

Enter FALSTAFF, SHALLOW, PETO, BARDOLPH,
and the Page.

Fal. Stand here by me, master Robert Shallow [*to* SHALLOW.] : I will make the king do you grace : I will leer upon him, as he comes by; and do but mark the countenance that he will give me. Come here; stand behind me. O, if I had had time to have made new liveries, I would have bestowed the thousand pound I borrowed of you. But it is no matter; this poor show doth better: this doth infer the zeal I had to see him.

Shal. It doth so.

Fal. It shows my earnestness in affection.

Shal. It doth so.

Fal. My devotion.

Shal. It doth, it doth, it doth.

Fal. As it were, to ride day and night; and not to deliberate, not to remember, not to have patience to shift me.

Shal. It is most certain.

Fal. But to stand stained with travel, and sweating with desire to see him: thinking of nothing else; putting all affairs else in oblivion; as if there were nothing else to be done but to see him. * * *

Shal. 'Tis so, indeed.

Enter the KING *and his* Train, *the* CHIEF JUSTICE *among them.*

Fal. 'Save thy grace, King Hal! my royal Hal! 'Save thee, my sweet boy!

King. My lord chief justice, speak to that vain man.

Chief J. Have you your wits; know you what 'tis you speak ?

Fal. My king! my Jove! I speak to thee, my heart!

King. I know thee not, old man : fall to thy
    prayers ;
How ill white hairs become a fool and jester!
I have long dream'd of such a kind of man,
So surfeit-swell'd, so old, and so profane ;
But, being awake, I do despise my dream.
Make less thy body, hence, and more thy
    grace ;
Leave gormandizing ; know the grave doth
    gape
For thee thrice wider than for other men :
Reply not to me with a fool-born jest ;
Presume not that I am the thing I was :
For Heaven doth know, so shall the world per-
    ceive,

That I have turn'd away my former self;

So will I those that kept me company.

When thou dost hear I am as I have been,

Approach me ; and thou shalt be as thou wast,

The tutor and the feeder of my riots :

Till then, I banish thee, on pain of death,—

As I have done the rest of my misleaders,—

Not to come near our person by ten mile.

For competence of life I will allow you,

That lack of means enforce you not to evil ;

And,·as we hear you do reform yourselves,

We will, according to your strength and quali-

tics,

Give you advancement.—Be it your charge,

my lord,

To see perform'd the tenor of our word.

Set on.   [*Exeunt* KING *and his* Train.

    Fal. Master Shallow, I owe you a thousand
pound.

    Shal. Ay, marry, Sir John ; which I beseech
you to let me have home with me.

Fal. That can hardly be, master Shallow. Do not you grieve at this; I shall be sent for in private to him: look you, he must seem thus to the world. Fear not your advancement; I will be the man yet that shall make you great.

Shal. I cannot well perceive how; unless you should give me your doublet, and stuff me out with straw. I beseech you, good Sir John, let me have five hundred of my thousand.

Fal. Sir, I will be as good as my word : this that you heard was but a colour.

Shal. A colour, I fear, that you will die in, Sir John.

Fal. Fear no colours; go with me to dinner. Come, lieutenant Peto;—come, Bardolph :—I shall be sent for soon at night.

Re-enter the CHIEF JUSTICE, Officers, &c.

Chief J. Go, carry Sir John Falstaff to the Fleet; Take all his company along with him.

Fal. My lord, my lord,—

Chief J. I cannot now speak: I will hear you soon. Take them away.

> [FALSTAFF, *after a pause, walks away as the curtains close.*

THE END.

LONDON:
WM. H. ALLEN & CO. PRINTERS, 13, WATERLOO PLACE, S.W.—L.

www.ingramcontent.com/pod-product-compliance
Lightning Source LLC
Chambersburg PA
CBHW030617030726
47497CB00006B/1536

* 9 7 8 3 3 3 7 1 0 5 9 1 4 *